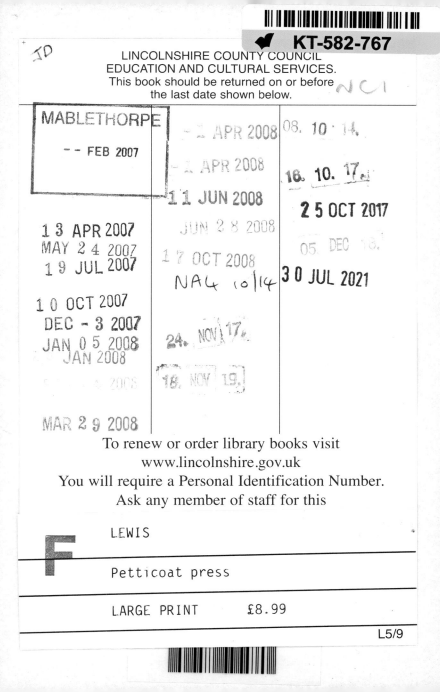

F

LEWIS

Petticoat press

LARGE PRINT   £8.99

L5/9

PETTICOAT PRESS

It's 1901, and Eleanor Paton has ambitions to become a journalist, so she is devastated when her father appoints Stephen Walsh as the new editor to his newspaper. Stephen refuses to print her articles. Eleanor is determined to succeed, but a dangerous connection with a militant suffragette causes errors of judgement in her work. However, as her talent begins to flourish under Stephen's guidance, a family crisis threatens to part them forever — just when they have fallen in love.

SHEILA LEWIS

PETTICOAT PRESS

Complete and Unabridged

LINFORD
Leicester

First published in Great Britain in 2005

First Linford Edition
published 2006

British Library CIP Data

Lewis, Sheila
   Petticoat press.—Large print ed.—
   Linford romance library
   1. Women journalists—Fiction
   2. Suffragists—Great Britain—History—Fiction
   3. Love stories 4. Large type books
   I. Title
   823.9'14 [F]

ISBN 1–84617–566–6

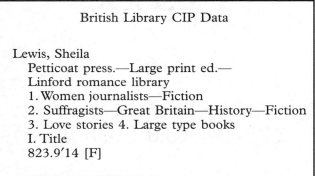
Published by
F. A. Thorpe (Publishing)
Anstey, Leicestershire

Set by Words & Graphics Ltd.
Anstey, Leicestershire
Printed and bound in Great Britain by
T. J. International Ltd., Padstow, Cornwall

This book is printed on acid-free paper

1

Eleanor Paton made her way along Colliers' Row in defiance of her father. He had advertised in his own weekly newspaper, *The Kessog Chronicle* for a live-in servant, and had given Eleanor strict instructions to conduct the interviews in the Paton home, as he was in England reporting on the funeral of Queen Victoria.

Eleanor decided to take advantage of his absence and see for herself the living conditions in this part of the town of Kessog, while interviewing a local applicant.

January 1901, had been a bitter month and the muddy surface of Colliers' Row had frozen the ground into rutted tracks. Her fine leather boots did not grip well and she stumbled along looking for the right address. To her the cottages looked no better than hovels crouched in the shadow of the pit's winding gear.

'Are ye lookin' for me?'

Eleanor looked up and saw a girl standing in an open doorway. She was of sturdy build, taller and broader than Eleanor herself, but her open face looked honest.

'Bethia Ogilvie?' Eleanor asked.

The girl nodded and held open the rough wooden door of her home. Inside, the main room was dark, the earth floor hidden by shabby rugs. From a corner came the sound of a baby whimpering and Eleanor caught a glimpse of a gaunt woman bending to hush it.

Eleanor, conscious of her ill-advised intrusion, hurriedly outlined the duties that would be required of the servant. 'It will be hard work. There are four of us, my father and my younger sisters. Father's shirts are of prime importance, the ink on his cuffs is the devil to clean,' her voice faded at this point. What was ink compared to the conditions which

Bethia was living in.

She was surprised to see a sympathetic gleam in Bethia's eyes. The girl understood her embarrassment. That gesture somehow convinced Eleanor that this girl would be worth having. When Bethia agreed to the suggested wage with a dignified nod, Eleanor warmed to her even more.

'Can you start tomorrow at six?' she asked. 'One day off a month.'

Eleanor left, pleased with her achievement. She crossed the bridge over Kessog Water that was the dividing line between poverty and wealth in the town.

'Eleanor!'

She jumped at the sound of the authoritative voice. Her former school teacher, Miss Dene, was waiting for her, the ferrule of her umbrella tapping on the ground.

'Whatever have you been doing in Colliers' Row?' then her expression changed. 'Going to write in the newspaper about conditions there?'

Eleanor gasped. How did Miss Dene know . . . ?

'Those letters in the *Chronicle* published under the pseudonym, James Gillies, are written by you,' the teacher declared. 'You should have known that I'd recognise your writing style. After all, I taught you.'

'You must not tell anyone,' Eleanor began in a panic. 'Certainly not Papa!'

Miss Dene snorted. 'Typical man of his generation. Completely short-sighted. You should have gone to university. Anyway, I've been looking out for you. I want you to put your talent for writing and passion for social justice to better use. Introduce women's suffrage to the paper.'

Eleanor was appalled. Papa would never publish letters on that subject. He was completely loyal to the old Queen who had disapproved of votes for women.

'I'll draft out something and you can write it up,' Miss Dene gave her a quick nod and strode on her way.

Eleanor moved on, her legs trembling. Apart from anything else, Papa naturally assumed the writer of the *James Gillies* letters was a man. He'd never allow women's words in print. When first her mother's illness and then her passing had restricted Eleanor to their home, she had suggested that she train as a reporter for the paper.

His disdain had been demeaning. 'Newspapers are not fit places for women.' He had no intention, he said, of *The Kessog Chronicle* being reduced to a 'petticoat press.'

Her sister, Clara, was waiting in the hall of Gowanbank on Eleanor's return, her face set in a mulish expression. She had inherited their mother's beauty of oval face framed by golden hair. At the moment the large blue eyes were flinty.

'About time, too. If this servant is not suitable I shall have to inform Papa of your underhand methods of recruitment,' Clara's voice grated. 'And Martha has had one of her accidents. I was forced to make her tea. The doctor should attend.' And with that she minced off upstairs, clutching her prayer book.

Clara had recently joined an evangelist group and with a great sense of her own importance, now viewed herself as the spiritual saviour of the house.

It appeared that Martha had fallen in the garden. At fifteen, she had the sweetest nature of the whole family, but was prone to accidents and illness. She was lying on the sofa, her face pale and pinched.

Since Eleanor could not remove the boot from Martha's swollen ankle, she did indeed have to send for Dr Fraser, the family physician.

Fortunately the good doctor, a handsome and benign man in his late fifties, was not accompanied by his medical student son, Lorne. He and Eleanor were sweet on each other, but their secret glances and kisses had to remain hidden, especially from Clara.

'Hot and cold compresses, my dear Eleanor,' Dr Fraser said on examining

Martha. 'Complete rest for a week, I'm afraid,' he touched Eleanor's shoulder gently. They both knew that all the care of Martha would fall on Eleanor's shoulders, as had been the case with her mother.

Two days later it seemed as if Bethia had been with them for months. It had taken barely a morning for the girl to read all the natures of the family. Eleanor knew that she commanded respect, Clara would have all her needs attended to without any degree of warmth, but Martha had enslaved the miner's daughter instantly.

On the evening of her second day, Bethia announced that a gentleman had called to see Eleanor. 'He has message from your father in London.'

Much concerned, Eleanor hurried downstairs to the parlour. When she entered the man was standing with his back to her. He was tall, wearing a serge suit, not of especial quality and it hung loosely on his frame. His hair, dark as peat, was untidy and in need of a barber's attention.

He turned at the sound of her step. She noticed that his face was narrow with prominent cheek bones and his eyes were dark as his hair. His full mouth was firm, but she sensed a tension there. It occurred to her that his face was one that had experienced suffering.

'Good evening, Miss Paton. I'm Stephen Walsh.' His voice was pleasing, softly accented with just the faintest trace of an Irish lilt. He seemed to be expecting a reaction from her so she gestured to a chair, assuming it wasn't a casual call.

'I met your father in England where I regret to say that he was taken ill,' his gentle tone softened the impact of the words, but still Eleanor was gripped by apprehension.

'Oh no! What has happened to him?' she cried.

'He suffered a seizure during the funeral procession, but he is recovering well in hospital in London. I was with him at the time and so able to accompany him.'

'Oh, thank you,' she said automatically. Poor Papa, how he hated being ill.

'I'm returning to London at the end of the week and will accompany him home by train,' Stephen Walsh assured her. 'He asked me to bring you the news and urged you not to worry.'

'Thank you,' she repeated. It seemed that Mr Walsh had taken care of everything, but one of his remarks made her question. 'You were with him at the time? Had you arranged to meet my father?' she asked.

He looked at her for a moment, then said: 'Yes. He had invited me to meet with him.'

It was only then that she noticed his hands — artistic, with slim bony fingers which were stained with ink. A sudden unease gripped her.

'May I ask why?' she asked.

Stephen Walsh hesitated for a moment. 'To discuss my appointment to *The Kessog Chronicle*.'

'I know nothing of this,' she said at once.

'Perhaps,' Stephen Walsh said hesitantly, 'Your father was reluctant to discuss business with you.'

Eleanor flushed. He was treating her like a child. He got to his feet. 'In the circumstances I am required to take over temporary editorship as soon as possible. Will you excuse me, Miss Paton?'

Eleanor sat, frozen into immobility. For a moment her father's illness was eclipsed by the fact that he'd employed a complete stranger to work on the paper without saying a word to her.

It was only after he left, that Eleanor realised the week's edition of the paper would be in Stephen Walsh's hands. What did he know of Kessog and the community? It was her duty to oversee his work until her father's return.

Early next morning she left all the household duties in Bethia's hands and walked briskly to *The Kessog Chronicle* building. It was prominently situated on the north side of Keir Square. The ground floor, the height of two storeys, held the huge rotary presses for printing the broadsheets. The din was deafening, but Eleanor revelled in the excitement of the steady mechanical beat and pungent smell of metal, ink and oil.

Stephen Walsh, his jacket hung over the back of her father's chair was discussing an item with the sub-editor and addressing him as, 'Doug.' Papa would be horrified at such informality.

After exchanging greetings, Eleanor wasted no time in getting to the point. 'I thought my father would be pleased if I advised you about this week's edition,' she said.

Stephen opened and closed his mouth a couple of times, rather like a fish, Eleanor thought, but then he said pleasantly, 'That's extremely thoughtful of you. Doug has set up the front page advertisements. My report on the Queen's funeral will be on page — '

'Your report?' she interrupted. 'I

thought you said my father took ill during the procession and that you accompanied him to hospital?'

He acknowledged her quick eye for detail with the merest flicker of an eyebrow. 'Quite true. I have to confess that the subsequent events were culled from the information of fellow journalists. It's a common practice, Miss Paton.'

'Hardly commendable.'

'But excusable in the circumstances.' There was a flash of reprimand in his eyes.

She hid her confusion. He had been assisting Papa. She leafed through some of the pieces laid on the desk, ready for printing.

'I don't see any of the letters from James Gillies. His contributions have found favour with our readers, and are highly esteemed by my father.'

'This week's contribution does not suit the edition. Besides, in my opinion they are the work of a female and thus not appropriate.'

Fortunately Eleanor's head was still bent over the desk and so he wouldn't see the flush of fury which washed over her face. She was quite unaware that her shoulders had stiffened noticeably. 'May I enquire as to your credentials, Mr Walsh?' She had her anger in check now.

'I have just returned from Africa where I have been reporting on the Boer War for a London newspaper,' he said.

'Isn't it rather climbing down the ladder to be editing a weekly provincial newspaper?' she challenged.

'Domestic circumstances have forced me to return from Africa. A colleague in London informed me of this position. Your father told me, when we met, that he wants to share the burden of producing the paper, due to recent ill health.'

Eleanor stared at him. Ill health? Papa had never mentioned feeling ill. But neither had he given a hint that he was meeting a prospective employee in

London. Until Papa returned home she had no option but to accept this bizarre situation.

★ ★ ★

One week later, Stephen and the coachman carried Henry Paton into Gowanbank. The older man was enveloped in an enormous greatcoat with a hat clamped on his head. The family caught only a glimpse of his face, putty-coloured, his features sunk and shapeless.

Once settled on the sofa, Eleanor rushed to his side, undid the coat and lifted the hat off his head. She kissed him and rubbed his icy-cold hands. There was no response. She then besieged him with questions which only provoked an irritable wave of his hands and she withdrew.

Clara and Martha then took her place at his side, each clucking and fussing. Stephen Walsh indicated to Eleanor that he wished to speak privately to her. 'I hoped you would be spared this, that your father's condition would have improved,' he spoke plainly. 'Unfortunately the seizure has robbed him of the power of speech. According to the doctors in London it is not known when, or if, he will recover it.'

Eleanor looked across at her father, her heart filled with pity. This was tragic — a disaster for a man who loved words, who revelled in discussions with his companions, whose whole life was based on communication.

⋆   ⋆   ⋆

Stephen walked back from Gowanbank to his rented cottage through a typical Kessog downpour. He wondered if he would ever get used to the rain in the West of Scotland.

He'd had little choice in choosing where to live when he'd returned from Africa in order to keep together what remained of his family. The town of Kessog, twenty miles south west of

15

Glasgow was part industrial with its colliery, textile mill and railway. It also served a large agricultural community.

Now he shared the cottage with his father's sister, Ivy Dunkers, who'd taken charge of his half-brother and sister. Jeffrey, aged fifteen and thirteen-year-old Amelia had been orphaned when Stephen's father and his step-mother had died in a railway accident in Kent.

Ivy had sent a telegram to Stephen in Africa stating she could only take care of the children if Stephen was there to support them all. He'd returned immediately and had taken the first offer of employment that came his way.

The cottage was situated at the end of an alley, known as Meikle's Land, which ran between a bakery and a funeral parlour. As he approached he saw the lamp burning in the cottage window. The curtains had not been drawn. That meant only one thing. Jeffrey had run away. It had been a frequent occurrence in London but

Stephen had hoped the boy would have had the sense to stay put in a strange town.

'Gone again,' Aunt Ivy clattered a saucepan on the range as Stephen entered the kitchen.

Amelia rushed over to throw herself into Stephen's arms. 'Please find him, Stephen. He really will get lost here in Scotland.'

'I'll do my best,' he promised the child, patting her soft brown hair.

'Not until you've had some hot food,' Aunt Ivy slapped a plate on the kitchen table and Stephen had to admit he was grateful for the meat pie and the scalding cup of tea which soon accompanied it.

Aunt Ivy was nearing fifty, a kindly, plump woman, a widow who'd never borne any children and was not yet used to motherly skills, beyond cooking excellent food and keeping house and children clean and tidy.

Jeffrey had made up his mind that 'going for a soldier' was the life for him.

17

Stephen had attempted to explain the horrors of harsh military life and of war to his half-brother, albeit a somewhat watered down version as he'd been reluctant to be entirely truthful about the agonies he'd seen in Africa. Jeffrey ignored all the warnings.

With a sigh, Stephen donned his already soaking coat and hat and left the cottage. As in London, he'd tour all the alehouses, or pubs as they were called in Scotland. Those were where the recruiting officers were to be found.

It was a fruitless search.

'It's yon Englishman, again,' was a comment he heard in every hostelry. He knew there was an antipathy to the English in this area yet he was determined to be accepted for what he was, no matter his nationality. Anyway, he was Irish by birth!

But they were only words. No outright hostility, due to the fact, he guessed, that Henry Paton had employed him. The newspaper owner was evidently a respected man in Kessog.

No-one admitted to having seen Jeffrey in any of the establishments, nor indeed any recruiting men. Stephen assumed that the boy had probably returned to the cottage.

As he plodded home again, Stephen's thoughts returned to the Paton family. It was clear that Henry expected Eleanor, as his eldest daughter, to be responsible for her sisters and the management of the household.

Even in his brief acquaintance with her, Stephen guessed that she had other plans and was ambitious. He'd detected a feminine mind behind the *James Gillies* letters, given their rather emotional tone, and it was clear from her reaction that she was the anonymous correspondent. He had to admit that they were well written, but she surely didn't plan to write for the newspaper? Her father would never permit it.

When he turned into the alley for the second time that evening he saw at once that the lamp was still burning in the window. The boy had not returned.

His heart sank. He had no idea where to turn next.

⋆　⋆　⋆

Eleanor's fingers were frozen into immobility as she watched Bethia attend to her father. She listened to his laboured breathing, the strangled gargle that came from his throat as he tried to communicate with them and felt powerless to help.

She had already been feeling guilty over her selfish thoughts about her writing when Papa was so ill, and at the same time terrified that her life was going to consist of nursing, yet again. She had not grudged one minute of taking care of her mother, scarcely allowing anyone else to help. Her love had been so fierce and her agony almost unbearable as she watched pain weaken and destroy the beautiful mother she so cherished.

Later, when she and Bethia had returned to the kitchen, she attempted to thank the girl. 'I'm happy to take care of him,' Bethia said immediately. 'I'm used to sickness in my home. Man or woman, makes no difference.'

Eleanor bit her lip. It wasn't fair that Bethia should be burdened by this. The girl was only seventeen, after all. 'You can't do everything,' she said. 'My sisters and I will help with the chores.'

'Someone to help with the washing would be good,' Bethia acknowledged. 'I know you'd help, Miss Eleanor, but there's plenty women in the colliers' cottages who'd be glad of the work, just for a few bawbees.'

She is so sensible, Eleanor thought, as I should be. Of course Clara would not lift a finger to help, and Martha would never be strong enough to be of any use.

'Fine,' she agreed. 'I'll leave it to you to organise that.' She wanted to hug the girl, but that would not be appropriate.

Bethia was the ideal person to nurse Papa. Had it been herself, it would have been fraught. He had never shown any special love for her, only wanted her to be a credit to him, as was typical of all Scottish families.

Soon after breakfast on Sunday morning, Dr Fraser returned to Gowanbank, this time accompanied by his medical student son, Lorne. He and Eleanor exchanged covert glances before father and son went upstairs to see Henry Paton.

Eleanor had coffee waiting for them when they returned to the parlour. 'How is Papa?' she asked at once.

'No improvement as yet,' Dr Fraser settled himself on the sofa. 'He isn't an invalid, though. He is able to get around and should be encouraged to do so. At the moment he seems in danger of withdrawing from everything.'

'There is a doubt about his speech returning,' Lorne said.

His father shot him an angry glance. 'That comment is premature and should not be mentioned.'

'Oh, I said nothing in front of Mr Paton, but I can interpret your diagnostic opinions,' Lorne was reclining in an armchair looking, in Eleanor's eyes, most devastatingly attractive.

'Early days yet,' Dr Fraser said firmly. 'However, my advice is that he does not return to work for the time being.'

'He will not like that,' Eleanor murmured.

At that moment, there came the tinkling sound of a hand bell, a device Bethia had thoughtfully put by Henry Paton's bedside in order that he could summon her without leaving his bed.

'I'll go up with the maid. I want to make sure that the sedative I administered is taking effect.' Dr Fraser rose and left the parlour.

At once Lorne crossed the room and caught Eleanor in his arms. 'I've missed you,' he said, then began nuzzling her neck. Eleanor forgot all about her father as her tension melted away, replaced by the thrill of his touch. Her body responded with an inner shudder that was excitingly disturbing.

Afraid that Clara might enter the

parlour at any time, Eleanor disengaged herself and took a step back from him. His eyes, blue-grey like the waters of a Highland loch, queried her action and she reached up and smoothed his thick blond hair.

'Clara,' she murmured.

'Bother her,' he snapped. 'We must meet again soon, very soon,' his eyes flashed with desire. 'Our secret place. Today, at four o'clock.'

'If it is possible,' she began, when there was a knock on the parlour door.

Bethia entered and announced that Mr Walsh had called to see Mr Paton. Stephen, weary after a sleepless night worrying about his brother's where-abouts, had decided to call on Henry Paton as early as possible.

He noticed at once that Eleanor looked better, a delicate bloom on her thin face was giving it animation and a softening effect at the same time.

She rather hesitantly introduced him to a young man who was sprawling indolently on the sofa. Stephen received a barely courteous nod from Lorne Fraser who clearly couldn't be bothered to rise, and who thereafter blatantly dismissed Stephen as being of no interest.

'Lorne is the son of our doctor. He's studying medicine,' Eleanor's tone was proud and breathless at the same time.

He must certainly be the best dressed medical student in Scotland, Stephen observed sourly. His suit was the finest tweed and made to measure. A good barber had cut the thick fair hair to enhance the broad face rather than emphasise it. Stephen had never seen colder eyes in his life.

He reflected that Eleanor Paton deserved better than this rude popinjay.

His father was a different proposition entirely. Dr Fraser had a personal word with him, advising that Henry Paton should be kept stimulated where the newspaper was concerned, but prevented from doing anything physically tiring.

After the Frasers departed, Stephen

and Eleanor went to speak to Henry Paton. Stephen briefly outlined the plans for the week and Henry accepted them all with a nod, clearly too tired to make any form of dissent.

'I'll accompany Mr Walsh to the *Chronicle*,' Eleanor said. 'I can bring any correspondence home for you.'

Stephen's heart sank. He didn't want Eleanor there. Her presence would surely delay his search for Jeffrey. And he certainly didn't want her to know he had a runaway brother.

They set off in yet another shower, although this time it was soft rain, a 'smirr,' as he'd heard Doug describe it.

As they entered Keir Square, Stephen noticed a horse and cart outside the newspaper building. Two figures sat on the cart's seat, one protected from the elements by rough sacking, the other crouched, shivering.

As Stephen and Eleanor approached, the larger figure stood up, throwing off the sacking as if it was filmy gossamer. The man was built like a pugilist with massive shoulders and forearms.

'You'll be the brother, then?' the man shouted, shaking his whip at Stephen.

Only then did Stephen recognise the other figure as Jeffrey. 'What the devil?' Stephen ran forward.

'What's the matter?' Eleanor ran to keep up with him.

'That's my brother up there,' he flung the words over his shoulder.

As they reached the cart the man pushed Jeffrey off and the boy fell on to the cobbles. In an instant Stephen was by his side. Jeffrey's face was chalk white, his clothes were sodden and his eyes full of apprehension. Stephen helped him to his feet.

'What was that for?' Stephen shouted at the man.

'Bringing him to justice,' the coarse voice replied. 'He was hiding on my property, ready to steal or rustle. I beat it out of him who he was and where to find you.'

Stephen bunched his fists and stepped towards the man.

'Mr McAllister,' Eleanor's voice carried clear over the cobbles. 'Can we discuss this in the office?'

Stephen whirled on her, eyes blazing, but was halted by the warning look on her face.

Once inside the *Chronicle* office, Stephen sat Jeffrey in a chair and put his coat round the boy's shoulders. McAllister started to rant again, but was smoothly interrupted by Eleanor.

'Let's hear what Jeffrey has to say,' she said.

Hesitantly, and in low tones, Jeffrey said how he'd been chased out of town by some lads the previous evening, had lost his way and because of the rain took shelter in a barn. He hadn't wanted to disturb anyone so late and didn't think he was doing any harm.

McAllister said nothing, his lip curled between his whiskers. Before Stephen could accuse him of vicious behaviour, Eleanor spoke again. 'A natural mistake by someone new to Kessog,' she allowed barely a second for McAllister's sour reaction before she continued. 'A waiver of your advertising fees for a month should settle the situation?'

The farmer's small eyes showed a calculating gleam before he turned and glowered at Stephen. 'It won't be smoothed over so easy next time,' he threatened, then lumbered out of the office.

'I can't believe you said that!' Stephen exploded.

'Did you want him to involve the police?' she asked.

'McAllister is the guilty one!'

'Not in his eyes, and the police would take his side as Jeffrey was on his property without permission. I know this place and the people. McAllister is a vicious, but powerful man,' she paused and then turned to Jeffrey. 'I'm sorry you've had such an unpleasant welcome to Kessog.'

'You did that to save the *Chronicle*,' Stephen accused her, knowing that newspapers relied on the revenue from advertisements to survive.

'It was the only way I could think of to stop McAllister,' she explained. 'The only power available to me.'

Stephen saw the hurt in her eyes and was instantly remorseful.

'Why don't you take Jeffrey home? He needs a warm bed and dry clothes.' She was business-like again.

'Would you be kind enough to accompany us? I'd like you to meet my aunt and sister,' Stephen said by way of contrition.

Eleanor looked surprised, then glanced at Jeffrey. 'Yes, I'd like that. I should have done more to make you welcome in the beginning and acquaint you with Kessog's customs — and faults.'

Stephen was silenced. Eleanor Paton was not yet twenty, yet there was a maturity and kindness about her that was impressive.

2

Eleanor was given a dignified, but warm welcome, by Ivy Dunkers in the gloomy cottage in Meikle's Wynd. After brief introductions, Stephen took Jeffrey into a bedroom for a change of clothing.

Eleanor had noticed the relief on Ivy's face when Stephen appeared with Jeffrey, but the young Amelia had been tearful. 'Jeffrey first ran away to be a soldier so that he could go to Africa like Stephen,' she confided to Eleanor with earnest belief. 'Don't you think that was a wonderful brave idea?' The delicate face, pointed like a kitten's, had much the same playful innocence of expression.

Eleanor, whose knowledge of wars came mainly from history books, nodded and smiled.

'He still wants to be a soldier. My

31

mother would have been so proud of him,' Amelia continued. 'I think that's why he wants to fight for his country — in her memory.'

Walking home, Eleanor reflected on the morning's happenings. She had noted little about Jeffrey, other than that at fifteen he was a tall and handsome boy, but definitely surly with his brother.

While defending the boy against McAllister, she had indeed also been thinking of the *Chronicle* and Stephen's position. McAllister would keep quiet about the incident as some of his income depended on sales he made through the advertisements. It was possible, though, that Stephen would have more trouble with Jeffrey. Was he capable of running the newspaper and dealing with that family at the same time?

With Papa being so ill, it was up to her to protect the *Chronicle*. She decided to make enquiries about another editor just in case. She'd say nothing to her father, of course, but approach Uncle Charles in Glasgow first. He was manager of a bank there and bound to have good contacts.

Two days later she posted an anonymous letter to the *Chronicle*. No 'James Gillies' this time. Stephen would have to pay attention to this one.

When she entered the editorial office the following day she noticed the letter lying on her father's desk.

Doug Houston, the sub-editor, was with Stephen and she thanked him for visiting Papa the previous day. 'I'll not deny it was a shock to see him,' Doug couldn't finish the sentence. Whether it was from distress or the effect of the drink he'd obviously had already, wasn't clear.

Eleanor tried to be charitable and hope that the drink was helping him cope with the shock, but alcohol had always been a problem with Doug. She knew Papa didn't consider him reliable, but kept him on for his sub-editing skills. She gave him a brief smile as he left the office.

'I am not going to publish this article encouraging boys to join the militia,' Stephen threw her letter across the desk.

It hadn't occurred to her that he would identify it as hers. Perhaps she shouldn't have written it so soon after Jeffrey's escapade. 'Papa had printed many of my letters before. He said he likes the spirit of the content, not to mention the writing,' she countered.

'I am not printing this, Eleanor,' the response was adamant.

'I think you will. I am the proprietor's daughter.' The instant she uttered the words, she regretted them. 'I withdraw that,' she said before he could respond.

'Yes, I should hope so. I won't be blackmailed.' His long pale face was rigid with disapproval.

'How dare you!'

'I am not printing this, Eleanor, because it is inaccurate and far too emotional — and for the wrong reasons. I have been to war. You have not. You cannot imagine what it is like. You haven't seen the injuries, the mutilation, devastation, the . . . ' his voice trailed off.

Eleanor kept quiet.

'The climate in Africa,' he resumed after a moment. ' . . . dust in every crevice — clothing, the eyes, the very eyelashes, on the tongue, curves of the ear. Clothes smell, bodies smell, flies everywhere,' his voice was harsh for a moment, then sank again. 'Nowhere to escape, just miles and miles of space baking under relenting sun. An empty world filled only with screams and blood.'

His head drooped but not before she saw the pain in his eyes. He didn't need to say another word. She understood now. What mother would send a son to endure that?

★　★　★

Martha was fit again and Bethia had engaged a Colliers' wife to help her with chores in the kitchen, so Eleanor was able to ask her father's permission to visit her Aunt Flora in Glasgow. As ever, he waved his hands in dismissal.

Visiting her mother's sister was perfectly in order, but Lorne had persuaded Eleanor to meet him later in Kelvingrove Park. His lectures would be over for the day and they could have some time alone.

Gently deflecting her aunt's invitation to take part in a séance in order to contact her late mother, Eleanor explained that she needed the advice of her husband, Uncle Charles.

Her aunt was horrified to hear of Henry's illness and disturbed at Eleanor's tale of the new, unknown editor and his family troubles.

'I might need Uncle Charles to find me another editor,' she said.

'But Henry has chosen this one,' Aunt Flora pointed out.

Eleanor bit her lip. 'Yes, that's true, but if things go wrong . . . '

'It sounds to me as if that family

needs some social life to keep them out of mischief. Why don't you invite them for an evening. Uncle Charles and I will come and he can assess this Stephen Walsh.'

At once Eleanor felt ashamed of her suggestion. If anything, Stephen deserved some sympathy over his family problems. Surely he had to be given a chance.

She tried to explain this later to Lorne when they met in the park.

'Get rid of him, he's a liability,' he said shortly, while leading her off the path into the shelter of some bushes.

'But the *Chronicle* is the most important thing in my family's life. I need to be so careful not to make a mistake,' she stopped, aware of Lorne's hands moving over her body, his fingers fiddling with the buttons of her bodice. 'Lorne!'

'I'm sick of all this talk of your local rag,' he growled, then said sharply as she disengaged his hands from her bodice. 'What is the matter with you

37

Eleanor? There's no-one here to see us.'

'That's hardly the point, Lorne. I'm not a cheap girl to be fondled in public.'

'Oh, spare me the proprieties,' he sneered. 'I'm beyond tame kisses and cuddles. Show me how much you care.'

Eleanor felt her resolve wavering, but somehow this did not seem right to her.

Suddenly he flung away from her. 'Next month then.'

'What do you mean?'

'My father has bought me a flat in a townhouse, not far from here. I shall have my own rooms. We can be alone — no-one to see us. Then I'll know if you love me.'

Eleanor's return journey on the train to Kessog was far from tranquil. She had thought she had the ability to think out problems and find fair solutions. But Aunt Flora had put a different perspective on Stephen's family difficulties.

The situation with Lorne was disturbing her too. She knew she was besotted with him, but their romance didn't seem to be following her idea of two people in love sharing everything. He seemed only interested in physical contact.

How she wished her mother were still alive. Aunt Flora proclaimed herself a medium and was anxious to try and put Eleanor in touch with her mother. Eleanor did not believe in contacting the spirit world, but she sorely needed someone to guide her at the moment.

Had Clara known that Stephen Walsh's brother was so handsome she would have worn her cerise silk instead of the grey wool gown on the evening of the dinner. It didn't seem to matter, though, as he was transfixed by her beauty from the moment he entered the parlour.

Stephen noticed the attraction, and while he thought Clara a vain coquette, the friendship might prove beneficial to his family. In effect, Jeffrey might change his mind about running away.

Ivy Dunkers and Eleanor's aunt, Flora Cleland, had lost no time in forming a friendship too, both being of similar age and childless, they discussed the problems of raising children.

Stephen felt himself relax and decided to enjoy the dinner, especially as he had been seated beside Dr Fraser. 'I'm amazed at the improvement in Mr Paton's appearance,' Stephen opened the conversation.

'He's in good hands in this house,' the doctor replied. 'Bethia is a sensible girl for one of her kind, and Eleanor keeps her father's mind stimulated by reading to him every day.'

Stephen glanced down the table at Eleanor. He hadn't thought she and her father were particularly close, yet reading to him was surely more beneficial and thoughtful than Clara's much advertised and voluble pious prayers.

He let his eyes rest on Eleanor for longer. Her hair was neatly dressed as suited her rather classically narrow features. Her eyes were remarkable, dark green and attractively luminous.

'The *Chronicle* seems to be ticking over fine,' Dr Fraser addressed his remark to Henry, but gave a nod in Stephen's direction.

Stephen was initially irritated by the 'ticking over' epithet, but then recognised it was a tactful approach in view of Henry's present inability to run the paper. They began to discuss current news in the area, in particular the proposed railway extension from Kessog to Newcrofts, a village on the other side of Meikle Hill.

Once the gentlemen retired to the library for Port and cigars, Stephen decided to stay with the older men. Lorne Fraser was pointedly ignoring him and Jeffrey was engrossed in a book.

Dr Fraser, concerned about his patient, soon escorted Henry up to bed. Charles Cleland immediately engaged Stephen in quiet discussion.

'The *Chronicle*'s finances are dealt with by my bank in Glasgow, as I expect you know,' he said.

Stephen nodded. There was such a morass of matters to attend to at the newspaper office, but he did remember Eleanor mentioning the banking arrangement.

'You will have noticed that the income is falling short of expenditure, due to the fact that several advertisers are late with their payments,' Charles continued.

'I'll attend to that first thing on Monday,' Stephen said, trying to control a rising panic. One discrepancy might be caused by the waiver of McAllister's advertising rates that Eleanor had insisted on. But the rest?

'Henry used to look after that side of the business too,' Charles had not taken his eyes from Stephen's face.

'It's taking me a little time to achieve all that Henry executed with such ease,' Stephen confessed.

Suddenly Charles Cleland's attitude changed. 'Aye son, I appreciate that, but from the look of him Henry's never going to be much use to you now.'

Stephen was shocked at his directness.

'Anyway, I read the paper regularly

and I like your style and your opinions,' Charles went on. 'But there's trouble ahead if you don't get someone to supervise the accounts.'

Back in the parlour, Martha and Amelia were curled up in the window seat, watching the scene as the men returned to join the ladies. Jeffrey made straight for Clara and showed her the book of poetry he'd been reading in the library.

'She'll ask him to join the 'Vangies',' Martha whispered.

'What's that?' Amelia was mystified.

'The evangelists, they meet every week to sing and pray. I have to go with Clara,' Martha grumbled.

'Well, our Jeffrey's gone all soppy over her,' Amelia said.

Lorne had positioned himself by the fireplace and now stared directly into Eleanor's eyes. 'Tuesday then. Kelvingrove Park and I'll take you round to see my rooms. Not ready for occupancy yet, but we can make plans.'

Eleanor's heart leapt. Plans! Did he

mean for the future, for marriage? What else?

'I'll try to come, Lorne,' she said, quietly breathless. 'But I need Papa's permission and I still have the responsibility of the newspaper.

Lorne's eyes darkened. 'For goodness sake, stop trotting into the *Chronicle*'s office every day. The town is beginning to talk. McAllister is not one to keep his mouth shut,' he hissed. 'Anyway, a newspaper is no place for any girl of mine. Wake up to the fact your writing is just an idle fancy.'

* * *

Stephen established a good working relationship with Doug Houston, the sub-editor, but such was the pressure of work that he hadn't given the chap much thought. Now as they sat opposite each other across the editor's desk, Stephen noticed that the contours of Doug's round face were sagging, the whites of his eyes were bloodshot, and his hair was in need of a barber's sharp scissors. His suit was badly stained into the bargain.

'We need to sort out the accounts,' Stephen said.

'Aye, we do,' Doug said, tapping his pipe on the edge of the fireplace's iron gate. 'But Mr Paton always dealt with them.'

Stephen frowned, disturbed by Doug's carelessness.

'Maybe Eleanor could help you out,' Doug said. 'She's keen enough to work here and it would keep her mind off writing things.'

It was a possibility that Stephen had considered, but he wouldn't dare to suggest it to Eleanor as an alternative to writing.

'I'll be off to follow up that story about the Member of Parliament coming to speak at the Town Hall.' Doug slid off his chair and was out of the office in a flash.

Stephen moved to the window to check just exactly where Doug was headed. He suspected it could be the pub across the square. Doug didn't seem able to face the day without some alcohol. Stephen reckoned it would be the man's downfall, sooner or later.

He lost track of Doug as he spotted Eleanor approaching the newspaper office. His heart lifted although he wasn't quite sure why that should be. She carried her umbrella, not over her arm, but rolled and held like a spear. That, coupled with her determined stride, told him she was in a resolute mood. He sensed she would want to talk about writing for the paper again.

He would be the first to admit that she could write well. All she needed was some training and he would be happy to supply it. But what would be the point? Her father would never agree. Maybe Doug's idea would make her feel she was contributing to the running of the *Chronicle*.

They exchanged pleasantries when she entered the office. He thanked her again for inviting his family to Gowanbank. From there it was easy to introduce the subject of Charles Cleland's concern over the accounts.

'I see McAllister took me at my word and hasn't paid,' Eleanor said, flicking through the unpaid accounts that Stephen had laid on the desk. 'Mmm, I see Dunlop and McIver have not paid either. They're cronies of McAllister and grudge every penny spent, even when it's for their own good.'

'Can you deal with those since you know the people?' he asked.

She shot him an angry glance. 'You think this happened because I gave McAllister the waiver.'

'Not necessarily and I'm grateful that you did, saving Jeffrey from disgrace, however unwarranted.' He paused. 'Until I am better acquainted with all the editorial duties I wondered if you would help with the accounts.'

'Me? A clerk! Looking after accounts?' she flared up.

'I just thought, well, you haven't been writing recently.' He could have bitten out his tongue.

'Oh, but I have! Writing is what I do. In fact I think it's time for me to have a place in this paper. For instance, a column entitled, *From Our Lady Correspondent*.'

Stephen just stopped himself from putting his head in his hands in despair. This was impossible! 'The time is not right for a lady correspondent in Kessog,' he said quietly.

Her eyes narrowed. 'Really? Are you as narrow-minded as all men?'

'Your father would not permit it,' he grasped at the excuse.

'He would never know. My name need not appear.' She leaned back across the desk. 'Set me a task. Give me an opportunity. Let me report on an event. See then if you can deny me a place on the *Chronicle*!'

Stephen drew a long breath. Curse the girl. Well, he would meet her challenge! He thrust a handbill at her. 'Joseph Devenay, our local Member of Parliament is speaking at the Town Hall on Wednesday evening. Go along and bring me a report of the meeting the next day.'

Eleanor took the handbill, strode to the coat stand, snatched her coat, hat and umbrella in one mighty swoop and made a dramatic exit from the office.

Stephen Walsh did not know it but he would have two reports on his desk on Thursday morning. Miss Dene had asked Eleanor to attend and write a report on the meeting of the Kessog suffragettes. True, it was the same evening, but Eleanor was confident she could handle both reports.

3

It was bitterly cold all day on Wednesday, winter's last barb in early March. People scurried about town saying little, as each word uttered sent a puff of vapour into the air. By evening it seemed a fraction milder and inside the Town Hall it felt warm, probably on account of a large turn-out at the meeting.

Joseph Devenay was one of the new Labour Members of Parliament and the theme of his talk was more work for the men in the community. He was constantly interrupted from the floor.

'Decent wages!'

'What happens when we fall sick and there's no money?'

A good point, thought Eleanor. She had discovered that Bethia's father had been laid off on account of his poor health. She had insisted to Papa that the girl's wages be increased. Bethia looked after them all, nursing her father into the bargain.

'Safer working conditions!' was another cry.

Eleanor's pencil flew over her notebook. Devenay had a fine passionate flow to his speech and handled the audience with great command.

Round the corner from the Town Hall in Keir Square, Stephen heard Doug stumble up the staircase to the newspaper's office.

'There's been an accident at Balcutt Mill,' he said, falling into a chair. His eyes were bleary as he fumbled in his pocket for his pipe.

Stephen had been on the point of leaving the office. He intended to have a quick meal then make his way to the Town Hall. He wasn't happy about Eleanor being on her own. He reckoned there would be a rough crowd at the Hall. 'Go home, Doug,' he said briskly. 'I'll report on the accident.'

'No, no,' Doug tried to rise, failed,

then succeeded at the second attempt. 'This is my job. I want to be there.'

Stephen hardened his heart. Maybe shock would bring Doug to his senses where his job was concerned. He'd go along with him just to make sure he could handle the report, then he'd cut back to the Town Hall.

Outside the air was raw, the sky dun-coloured. Despite his greatcoat, Stephen shivered. Three months ago he'd been sweltering in the dry heat of South Africa.

A thin film of ice cast menacing reflections from the meagre lamps which lit the regimented windows of Balcutt Mill. Men and women were surging round the entrance.

'Stand clear!' came a stentorian shout. 'Doctor's here.'

The crowd parted and Stephen saw Dr Fraser hurry into the building. 'What happened?' Stephen spoke to the man nearest to him.

'Don't know yet,' was the growled reply.

'My bairn is in there.' This time a wail from a shawled woman.

'What's your bairn doing in there?' Stephen demanded.

'Workin' — what else? My man died last year. Now the lad's on one shift, me on the next. Ah've another four bairns at home.'

Stephen was ashamed of his question. Life was hard for these people. Her son was probably no more than fourteen, might even be only twelve.

He looked round for Doug, but he was nowhere to be seen. He'd have to handle this on his own. He pushed through the crowd to the mill entrance which was now barred by two police-men. 'I'm able-bodied and strong,' he said to one of them. 'Is any help needed?'

The policeman started at him. 'Got family in there?'

As Stephen shook his head the policeman stood aside and shouted above the protest from the crowd. 'He's been sent for by Dr Fraser!'

At first Stephen could see nothing. The air inside the mill was dust laden. The sound of voices and weeping drew him to the far corner where the mill had been built deep into the hillside which rose above the river.

He could only discern a massive jumble of wood, hopelessly inter-mingled with bundles of clothing. A group of men were bent over, pulling at the heap, lanterns swinging above their heads, casting grotesque shadows on the walls but not the ceiling. The ceiling had disappeared.

It was clear that part of the floor above had given way, tumbling looms and workers down on to the looms and workers on this floor.

No-one spoke, save Dr Fraser giving instructions as to where and how to lay the injured until he could attend to them. Everyone was aware of the danger of further collapse from above.

★　★　★

Joseph Devenay had now reached the stage in his address where he repeated the phrases, 'Leave that to me, I make a promise here tonight that I will . . . ' Eleanor decided that he was bringing the meeting to a close. She tilted her fob watch and read the dial. Eight forty-five. Just nice time to reach Miss Dene's house for the suffragette meeting.

Many men were on their feet now, heckling Devenay. It was easy to slip out. As she reached the door, she heard the words, 'railway' and 'gangers' shouted at the platform, and hesitated. Would something significant come up? Probably not.

Outside it was deadly quiet. Then the first snowflake drifted downwards. Eleanor scurried along Station Road to Wood Lane and Miss Dene's cottage.

*   *   *

Four dead, nine injured. It took two hours to bring everyone out. Stephen walked out of the mill with a weary but angry Dr Fraser.

'Place is a disgrace,' the doctor said. 'Dampness everywhere. The mill should never have been built into the hill. No air circulates. Floorboards have been rotting away for years by the look of it.'

'Are there no regulations to govern places like this?' Stephen asked.

The answer was a short. 'Somebody needs to run a campaign to expose the greed of owners of places like this,' he glanced at Stephen. 'Somebody like you with the power of the word and the facility to publicise it.'

'I take your point,' Stephen was already mentally composing his account of the accident and the apparent causes.

Outside it was deathly quiet. At first the brightness didn't register with him. He thought it was the contrast with the dim interior of the mill. But as soon as he put his feet down his shoes sank into a carpet of snow.

He bade the doctor goodnight and

trudged towards the Town Hall. He heard the noise long before he reached it.

The steps of the hall were swarming with people, shouting and screaming. It was more than just a political argy bargy. Arms were being swung, fists flaying everywhere and people began to fall over like ninepins.

Stephen launched himself into the crowd. Where in God's name is Eleanor? He started screaming her name, unaware it sounded like a keening wail, only knowing he couldn't bear it if anything had happened to her.

Miss Dene's cottage looked blank even with the covering of snow. A light was barely visible through the curtained window. Eleanor felt a sense of mystery, or perhaps concealment.

The door opened instantly at her knock and Miss Dene ushered her into the living-room. 'This is our writer,' she said to the women in the room.

Eleanor heard her words with a mixture of pride and trepidation. Would she be able to satisfy this group with her work?

She had to conceal her surprise on recognising most of the ladies present. They were all related to prominent men in Kessog, among them the Provost's wife and the mother of the Minister of Kessog Church.

'We meet secretly, Eleanor. Not because we are ashamed of the cause,' an elderly lady said. 'But some Kessog folk would shun and ridicule us without giving us a chance to prove that we can achieve a better life for women once we have a voice in Parliament.'

'In the meantime we organise support for our less fortunate sisters by means of benefit funds,' Miss Dene said.

Eleanor immediately thought of Bethia and the other families who lived in Collier's Row. The cause would surely benefit them. Then she became aware that the ladies were waiting for a response from her.

'Your good work should not go

unacknowledged,' she said firmly.

'You see, ladies, I told you Eleanor would publicise our ideals,' Miss Dene said.

'Make sure you let people know what we are about. I have no time for mealy-mouthed approaches,' another younger, harsher voice spoke.

Eleanor recognised Robina Insch, who served behind the counter at the co-operative shop on the opposite side of Keir Square from the *Chronicle* building. She was a tall handsome woman, around thirty, with a cool, distant manner.

'We resolved on no militant action,' Miss Dene said sharply.

'I know you can't do anything or you'll lose your position,' Robina was unable to keep an echo of derision from her tone. 'Just leave the protest to me!'

'No, Robina,' the voice of the minister's mother was steel in a velvet glove.

'We call ourselves the Sisters of Unity and plan to join one of the major suffragism societies in Scotland,' Miss Dene told Eleanor.

'Can we count on you as one of us, Eleanor?' another lady asked.

'I'd be honoured,' she said.

She took up her note-taking again while Miss Dene told the group that the new Member of Parliament supported them. 'Mr Devenay is in favour of universal suffrage.'

'It's a pity the whole government isn't of the same mind, and I can't say I regret the passing of the old Queen,' another lady said. 'She disapproved of women's enfranchisement. Probably set the cause back forty years when she might have helped us so much.'

By the time Miss Dene drew the meeting to a close, Eleanor had a mass of information on the projects to be undertaken by the Sisters.

She trudged home through the snow, her brain alive with excitement. She was now a suffragette, prepared to fight for the rights of women. Papa, Lorne and Stephen presented her with an uphill struggle given their narrow views of her place in the world. But this was a new century, a new era.

Martha had caught a fever the previous evening while attending the Evangelists' meeting with Clara, Jeffrey and Amelia, and so next morning Eleanor sent for Dr Fraser but was thrilled at first when Lorne arrived.

He made clear his irritation at having to attend to her sister. 'Martha seeking attention as usual,' he complained. 'Father's much too busy to visit. He is treating some accident victims at the hospital. Give her some cough mixture. You must not send for us over trifles like this, Eleanor.'

'She is my responsibility. Next time I'll call a horse doctor for her cough,' she said lightly as they descended the staircase.

Lorne pushed her into the parlour then caught her up in his arms. 'My fiery love,' he brushed her lips with his. 'I only want to save you needless anxiety. Anyway, I was glad of the excuse to see you.'

Eleanor fixed on the term 'love'. He must care for her.

'Meet me tomorrow in the park. I have some special news for you,' he kissed her again and left.

Eleanor spent the rest of the morning working on her accounts of both political meetings. She had written up as much as she could the previous evening, but now wanted to make sure she had not forgotten any detail.

After lunch she set off for the *Chronicle* offices. As she entered, she thought Stephen looked tired. She asked if he had had a late night.

'Busy,' he replied shortly, then paused as if waiting for her to speak. 'There was an accident at Balcutt Mill,' he finished eventually.

She remembered Lorne mentioning that his father was at the hospital treating accident patients. 'Was it a bad one?' she asked.

He succinctly gave her the details in a flat voice.

Eleanor's throat dried up with shock. She'd visited the mill once as a child with her father when he was writing a feature on it. In her mind's eye she tried to picture the collapse of those ranks of looms. It was terrifying.

'I don't expect you heard about it, being at the Town Hall meeting of course,' Stephen said.

She took the pages of written paper from her bag. Perhaps reading it would take her mind off the accident. She passed over her report. Without looking at her, he began reading.

It was a shock when he contemptuously threw it down on his desk. 'That is your complete account of the evening?' he asked, unsmiling.

'Isn't it good enough?' she bristled.

'As far as it goes. But it is incomplete.'

'What do you mean?'

By way of answer he picked up a copy of the *Glasgow Herald* and showed her the headline.

RIOT AT KESSOG. MEMBER OF

PARLIAMENT ATTACKED ON TOWN HALL STEPS.

Eleanor was appalled. At once she remembered the rumble of dissent when the subject of the railway extension had been raised just as she was quitting the hall. She knew at once she had failed Stephen.

'Were you really there, or is your report just a fictitious account?' his earlier flat tone had flared into vibrant anger.

'I do not write fictitious accounts. My account is a true representation of what Mr Devenay said. I was there!'

'What he said while you were there,' the sensitive mouth she had once admired was now a thin line. 'Your account is incomplete, therefore inaccurate and irresponsible.'

'I . . . I didn't think there was going to be any trouble,' she muttered.

'You left before the end?'

'It was about to end,' she protested.

'You missed the real news point, do you understand that, Eleanor? A good reporter doesn't leave until the last person goes home.'

'I'm sorry.'

'That isn't good enough,' his anger had returned. 'How can I trust you when you can't be bothered to endure the whole meeting. If we were a daily paper competing with the Glasgow one we would have failed our readers. Why did you leave?' he asked when she remained silent.

Eleanor felt she couldn't betray the Sisters' anonymity at this point. They had all asked not to be named in her report. She kept silent.

'I see, no doubt you took the opportunity to have a secret rendezvous with that supercilious medical Lothario!'

Appalled at his remarks, and already undermined by her lack of professionalism, Eleanor's courage deserted her and she fled from his office.

Stephen slumped down in his chair, the imagine of Eleanor's stricken face imprinted on his mind. How could he have been so cruel to her? That jibe about Lorne Fraser sprang from pure jealousy.

Devastated by the horrific mill accident, followed by the desperate search for Eleanor among the rioting men outside the Town Hall had left him emotionally drained. But she hadn't deserved his nasty barbs.

The rioters had wanted Joseph Devenay to stop the railway company importing Irish gangers. As with many political gatherings, there were always some who relished a good fight, regardless of the cause.

It had been a restless night for him. When he couldn't find her at the hall he reckoned she must have got home safely, but he still had to come to terms with the shock of realising how much she meant to him. Still sunk in his brooding thoughts, it took a moment or two to realise that the office door was open.

Eleanor stood in the doorway. In a flash he was on his feet.

'I want to apologise . . . ' They spoke in unison.

Good manners insisted that he allow Eleanor to speak first. She approached his desk slowly, her face flushed and with an anxious look in the depths of her green eyes. 'I was completely unprofessional,' she spoke as if she had rehearsed her words. 'That won't happen again. It was selfish of me to leave Devenay's meeting for . . . '

He held his breath while she hesitated. Perhaps it hadn't been for Fraser after all!

'I went to another meeting,' she took a deep breath. 'A suffragette meeting. I was invited to write a report on their work and aims. It is hoped it might be published in a future issue of the *Chronicle*.'

For a moment Stephen was unable to speak. Despite her apology, her small frame was taut with tension and determination. It had taken great courage on her part to come back so soon, and make such a full and honest confession. He lowered his eyes. Perhaps his admiration for her was revealing more than he wished.

He then made his own apology. 'What I said to you was unforgivable,' he saw by the renewed flush on her face that she understood he was referring to his jibe about Lorne. 'I went along to the Town Hall intending to see you home safely. The fighting was in full swing when I arrived.'

Her eyes widened. 'You thought there might be trouble, that I could be hurt?'

He shrugged. 'I thought it possible.'

She sank down in the chair and covered her face with her hands. 'And this was after you'd been to the mill?'

Stephen stood up. 'Let's get out of here.' The office had become claustro-phobic, enclosed in emotion and accusations and distress.

They went to a small coffee house across the square. Stephen, at Eleanor's request, told her about the scene at the mill, describing it from a reporter's point of view.

She listened carefully, asking only relevant questions. In his opinion she would make a good reporter.

He was sympathetic to the cause of the suffragettes believing women should have the vote, being aware of their potential to work hard to better conditions. But he knew he was in the minority.

They finished their coffee and parted in the Square, Eleanor to return home and he to the office. He watched her walk at her usual pace, but her head was down. He hoped that, like him, she thought they had mended fences and maybe could begin a tentative friendship. With all his heart he wished it so.

Next day, Eleanor escorted Ivy Dunkers to her Aunt Flora's house in Glasgow. After a while she excused herself saying she had to fetch some books for Papa.

She hurried to Kelvingrove Park. Lorne was waiting by the copper beech and at once snatched at her hands then gave her a long kiss. 'That is a promise of better to come,' he announced.

Eleanor flushed but was secretly

delighted at his passionate talk.

'Father has agreed that I should take rooms in Glasgow,' he told her. 'Since it is my final year of study I need to be within easy reach of the Infirmary.'

Eleanor was dismayed. 'But we'll never meet if you live here!'

'My dear sweet dove, of course we will — and alone, in my rooms,' his tone was honeyed.

'Would that be correct?' she asked, then flushed again as he snorted. 'I do want to be with you, Lorne, but nothing must spoil the future for us.'

'Spoil the future?' He gave a short laugh. 'It will be years before we can afford to marry.'

'I realise you have more study ahead, but I might be earning too,' she said, hoping he'd be proud of her.

Without warning he dropped her arm. 'Don't tell me that Irish bog trotter has been filling your head with fancy ideas about writing,' he said scathingly.

Eleanor was stunned at his fury.

'Stephen Walsh thinks I can write,' she shot back at him. 'I'll be published before long.'

'No doubt this week's pages will be plastered with his heroic deeds.' Sarcasm dripped from his voice.

'What are you talking about?'

'He was at Balcutt Mill. It must have looked to father, who likes to believe good of everyone and is blind to charlatans, that Walsh was helping with the injured,' Lorne laughed disparagingly. 'I'm sure all he was after was a news story for your father's rag.'

Lorne's derogatory description of the *Chronicle* fuelled her anger. 'Why weren't you at the mill helping your father?' she asked with some asperity.

'Why should I do that? These people are their own worst enemies. I have set my sights a little higher than the peasants of Kessog,' he said loftily. 'We don't want weavers and miners at our dinner table, my love, do we?' He turned his melting smile on her.

Eleanor, confused by all the swings of

argument, allowed herself to be led along the path. She had to fight for so much these days and she wanted a little oasis of comfort and love.

Lorne was the only person who seemed to offer that.

4

May blossom had transferred Kessog into a town decked out in pink and white before Lorne moved into his rooms in Glasgow. The passage of time had also caused a gradual decline in Henry Paton's health.

Eleanor chafed at the sense of being a prisoner in her home, but it was her duty, although Papa was constantly irritable and found fault with every little thing she did.

It was Stephen who suggested that a move to a downstairs room would allow Henry to receive visitors and not feel so isolated. 'Your library overlooks the front garden and road, which would enable him to see passing folk and all his books will be to hand,' he said to Eleanor.

She readily agreed. Stephen was a most unusual man and kept surprising her in so many ways. Just when she was convinced that he was unfeeling, he would do something thoughtful.

A few days later Eleanor entered the kitchen to find a strange woman sitting at the scrubbed table. The woman hastily jumped to her feet at Eleanor's entrance. Bethia introduced her as her cousin, Lily Ross, and mentioned that she'd been helping with mending work.

Eleanor noticed Lily's scrawny frame and tense expression. Then she remembered why the name seemed familiar. This was the woman who had lost a son at Balcutt Mill.

'I was very distressed to hear of your loss,' Eleanor said.

A cloud passed over the woman's eyes but she merely gave a brief nod.

Eleanor knew that no compensation had been paid to any of the relatives of those killed and injured. She wondered how Lily Ross was managing to feed her other four children.

She asked her a few questions and formed the conviction that Lily was almost destitute. The poorhouse beckoned. 'I'd like to let the whole of Kessog know about this through the *Chronicle*,' she said.

'I don't want to get into trouble,' Lily said at once.

'You won't,' Eleanor assured her. 'It's those responsible that I'm after. And you'll be paid for speaking to me.'

'No need for that,' Lily bristled.

'It isn't charity,' Eleanor said. 'It will help sell the papers and . . . ' she added with total honesty ' . . . that helps my family, too.'

Eleanor fetched her notebook and undertook her very first interview.

Later in the day she was able to visit the newspaper offices. She handed Stephen her latest piece of writing. 'It's an interview with Lily Ross,' she told him.

'She wouldn't talk to me,' Stephen was amazed.

'I had the chance to speak to her at Gowanbank,' she explained. 'She has no regular money and four children to feed. Do you think we could force the mill owner to pay compensation?'

'I've been trying for that in my own articles without any success.' Stephen read the interview.

'I've never interviewed anyone before and it's probably pretty amateurish, but this is the type of case the Sisters of Unity want to help,' she said.

Stephen laid the papers on his desk. 'It is a good interview, Eleanor. You seem to have a natural aptitude for getting to the heart of people and their problems.' His voice was full of admiration.

'Then you'll publish it?'

'I want to, but your father will have to approve,' he reminded her 'Shall I say it's from 'James Gillies'?'

'No,' she was adamant. 'That's finished. I won't shelter behind a ghost figure ever again.'

'He's bound to ask me who wrote this. I already told him that Lily refused to speak to me at the time of the accident.' He pondered a moment. 'I could say it's from a lady correspondent who wishes to remain anonymous.'

She thought about the aims of the suffragettes. To remain anonymous was an example of the attitudes they were fighting. Women had to show they were equal in as many areas as possible. Would she be betraying those ideals by hiding?

Stephen spoke again. 'It's a matter of deciding whether to lose the opportunity to help another woman or not.' He had guessed her dilemma and she could see a shadow of sympathy in his eyes. Papa would not allow her name in print. It didn't take long to wrestle with her conscience. Above all, suffragettes were dedicated to helping women.

'Anonymous,' she told Stephen and was gratified to see a flash of warm approval in his eyes.

Then he surprised her. 'If you're happy to write under 'Anonymous' perhaps you'd like to undertake some local reports? Doug and I are pretty busy and . . . '

'I'll do it,' she barely let him finish his sentence.

He laughed at her enthusiasm. 'It will be short accounts, probably not more than a hundred words each time. Cattle auctions. An obituary. The opening of a new school.'

'I won't make mistakes and won't ask for a wage.' She bit her tongue. 'Oh, yes, I will ask to be paid.' She remembered she had just as much right as a man to a wage for her work!

'I'm hiring you.' Stephen had moved over to the window. She thought he was concealing a smile. 'I'll pay you.'

'If I am successful, I'll tell Papa everything,' she declared.

Stephen turned from the window. 'But in the meantime, we'll keep quiet. I don't like deceiving your father any more than you do, but I think you need to prove yourself first where he is concerned.'

She nodded. 'Where will I begin?'

Stephen looked a little nonplussed for a moment then said, 'Why not write an account of the Evangelists' meeting? Jeffrey and Amelia go along with your sisters. It must be interesting or Jeffrey would never stick it.'

It seemed a tame beginning to what she considered a new career, but she was wiser now. It would be a good idea to keep an eye on the youngsters anyway. Martha had told her recently that Clara and Jeffrey met after school.

There was no point in raising the subject with Papa. He doted on Clara, yet Eleanor felt it was quite wrong for her to be alone with a young man.

The Edenway Evangelists met in a converted barn tucked away at the end of Wood Lane. Eleanor was surprised by the warmth inside. Rugs were scattered on the stone floor and logs burned in a vast fireplace at the far end.

The ''Vangies', as they were known in Kessog, were led by Bruce Urquhart who ran a draper's shop in town. The members were comprised of people who had left the Church of Scotland over theological disagreements and others who adhered to no specific faith.

Bruce opened the meeting with a prayer and then, to Eleanor's astonishment, Clara led the singing, accompanied by a young girl on the piano. Clara had a sweet singing voice, with undoubted power, but Eleanor sat in her chair, rigid with shock and embarrassment.

Clara was revelling, not in the message of the hymns, not in giving sweetness and clarity to the music, but in the fact that she was the focus of the meeting. She crassly exaggerated every line with dramatic gestures.

Beside her, Eleanor heard subdued giggling. Even Martha and Amelia knew Clara was flaunting herself abominably. She looked at Jeffrey. The boy was bewitched by the performance.

Eleanor could not tell Papa. He would say she was making it up, thinking her jealous of Clara's beauty and tuneful voice. She could not tell Lorne. He would see it as demeaning. She could not tell Stephen. He might forbid Jeffrey attending the meetings and then it would be back to the recruiting men. Stephen didn't need that worry again.

★ ★ ★

It was Saturday afternoon, the *Chronicle's* weekly issue was in the hands of the readers and Stephen was relaxing in the baking scented kitchen at Meikle's Land. To his great relief, Aunt Ivy had offered to take care of the newspaper's accounts, as she'd had some experience of book-keeping before her marriage.

'What shall we do about Amelia?' Her sudden question astonished Stephen.

'I didn't know we had to do anything about her. She's only thirteen,' he replied.

'She doesn't apply herself to anything at the moment,' Ivy said. 'Not lessons, not housework, just giggles all the time with Martha Paton when she's here which is practically all the time.'

That seemed a sensible arrangement to Stephen, both girls out of harm's way. He honestly couldn't see a problem. But then he'd had little to do with Jeffrey and Amelia when they came with their mother on her marriage to his father. Then he'd been intent on building his career as a foreign correspondent and had not been interested in the children at all.

'Anything to eat?' Jeffrey swaggered into the kitchen just as Ivy removed a tray of scones from the oven.

'Hands off, young man,' she jerked the tray away from him and several scones toppled on to the floor. 'Now look what you made me do!'

'I didn't touch them, it was your own silly fault!'

'Apologise at once. How dare you speak to Aunt Ivy like that!' Stephen shouted at him.

Jeffrey whipped round. He hadn't noticed Stephen sitting at the table on the other side of the kitchen. An expression of dislike crossed Jeffrey's face. 'Not out selling newspapers?' he taunted.

'Apologise!' Stephen roared.

'Dweadfully sowwy, dear Aunt Ivy,' Jeffrey said in baby speak, tweaked an escaped strand of Ivy's hair and then with a movement so swift it took the others by surprise, scooped all the fallen scones from the floor and ran out of the kitchen.

Stephen slumped in his chair. He had no idea why Jeffrey should despise him so. It couldn't be only because he refused to allow him to join the Army. It had to be something deeper than that and his attitude had been evident from the very day Stephen had returned from South Africa.

He'd tried talking to Jeffrey, taking him out, introducing him to the complexities of the newspaper, office, to a football match in Glasgow, but the hostility never lessened.

He never suspected that his father had been so proud of him that he'd talked incessantly about his achievements to his step-brother. Jeffrey had had Stephen's brains, his exploits, his loyalty thrust at him from the moment his mother had married Dermot Walsh. All his step-father desired was that Jeffrey should become a son he could be proud of, as he was of Stephen.

He'd ended up hating Stephen and when he'd come home to be their guardian, Jeffrey could think of nothing but joining the Army and showing him he was somebody too.

'You haven't forgotten it is his birthday next week?' Ivy said.

'I remember,' he answered. 'Sixteen. Maybe I could marry him off.'

Ivy gave him a shocked look then realised he was being humorous. 'He's sweet enough on that Clara Paton, or so Amelia keeps telling me.'

It was probably due to Clara Paton that Jeffrey had stopped running away. Stephen didn't care for the girl, one or other would soon become bored, anyway, but in the meantime she was useful.

'Actually, Eleanor suggested we all might go to Glasgow to see one of those new cinematographs,' Stephen said.

'Oh, that would be wonderful,' Ivy clapped her floury hands. 'And it might please his lordship.'

It was worth a try, Stephen thought and at least he would have Eleanor's company.

Theatre managements had taken advantage of the cinematograph by giving a brief showing, sandwiched between musical hall acts. Unfortunately, the acts were offensive — vulgar and crude.

At the interval they all went out to the foyer to buy some ice-cream. 'I'm sorry, Eleanor, this is unsuitable for the family,' he said quietly.

'Yes, the show is in appalling taste,' she spoke with clear deliberation. 'The actresses and singers are behaving badly in a completely unladylike way.'

It took a moment or two for him to realise her words were directed at the girls, not him. 'I'd rather we didn't return for the rest of the programme,' she said.

'I agree. Would you mind taking the children home, Ivy?' Stephen asked.

'But we haven't seen the new cinematograph,' Martha wailed.

'Papa would be most upset if, after giving you permission to bring us, you failed to let us see the new invention,' Clara said, her face full of false innocence.

By the tightening of Eleanor's mouth, Stephen knew that she too had seen the blackmailing threat in Clara's answer. He was furious that his plan to spend some time alone with Eleanor had been thwarted. He was quite unaware that Jeffrey had been watching him closely and that his brother had correctly interpreted Stephen's reaction. He could hardly believe that Stephen was sweet on stuffy old Eleanor, but he secreted the knowledge. Who knew when it might be useful.

Martha didn't really care whether she saw the cinematograph but she wanted to be in Jeffrey's company a little longer. He had sat between her and

Clara and had noticed her at last.

And if she wasn't mistaken, Eleanor would soon be putting a stop to the 'Vangies meeting, or at least Clara singing there. Amelia and she had had such fun watching the horrified expression on Eleanor's face that night.

Since they had to endure the rest of the show, Eleanor decided to put the experience to good use. She constantly stressed to all the vulgarity of the performers and how degrading their performances were. Ivy and Stephen supported her without knowing the real reason behind her opinion.

Clara ignored her. She was studying the flamboyant attitudes of the actresses. Last summer Papa had taken them to an open-air theatre in Kessog Park. It was by copying the singers there that she had perfected her performance at the 'Vangies. She was well aware that Jeffrey never took his eyes off her.

But now! She watched the dipping of the shoulders, the coy looks, the swirl of skirts showing a flash of ankle, the extravagant bow to the audience. Yes, she could do all that. She supposed it was a form of temptation and only by recognising temptation could men reject it. Yes, that was her role at the 'Vangies.

After escorting the Paton girls home, Stephen's family returned to Meikle's Land. He asked them if they had enjoyed the evening. Jeffrey ignored the question and left the room, a knowing smile playing round his mouth.

'The cinematograph was wonderful,' Amelia was entranced.

'What about the singers and actresses?' he asked her.

'All right, I suppose,' Amelia replied. 'Clara prances about like that every week at the 'Vangies.'

Ivy folded her arms over her black bombazine bosom and nodded at Stephen as if she'd known all along.

⋆   ⋆   ⋆

Stephen watched Henry Paton's face as he read Eleanor's review of the cinematograph. She had written it in a lively style, suited as she had told Stephen, for all that was new in the century.

He knew that Henry assumed Stephen himself had written it. How he wished he could tell him the truth.

Eleanor had told him that she planned a full confession to her father one day. Stephen decided he would then make it clear to Henry that he personally had hired her, considering her work worthy of publication in the *Chronicle*.

When Henry nodded his approval of the review, Stephen took advantage of his good mood. 'I have another interesting article awaiting space in the paper which concerns new suffragette movement in Kessog.'

Henry shook his head vehemently.

'I have noticed that the Glasgow papers are giving the issue wide coverage,' Stephen commented.

He knew the older man was obsessed about competing with the Glasgow publications. Stephen was doing this partly for Eleanor's sake, but it also wouldn't do to let the *Chronicle* fall behind in reporting a progressive movement.

'I didn't write it myself,' Stephen went on, hoping he wouldn't be pressed for a name. He wanted to draw the line at an outright lie.

Henry indicated a grudging acceptance.

Stephen returned to the office in high spirits. He was looking forward to telling Eleanor the good news. The report was fairly mild in content the Sisters seemed bent on obtaining the right to vote to enable them to promote social welfare, and were being specific in the means they intended to use.

Eleanor's first reaction to the news that her article on the Sisters of Unity was to be published, was that she should immediately tell Miss Dene. Only that morning she'd received a letter from the schoolmistress complaining that Martha's school work was deplorable and she wished to discuss the matter.

However, she was distracted when

she left the newspaper building by the fact that Robina Insch was watching her from the co-operative shop doorway. She ran across the square and told her about the article.

'It's just the beginning,' Robina said, her cool, luminous eyes flaring with passion. 'Once everyone knows about us, they will have to recognise our rights,' she paused. 'Or we make them!'

Eleanor felt a wave of uneasiness flood her body. Robina was the only member of the Sisters that she'd been uncertain of. After being barred from all militant action, Robina had contributed nothing else to the meeting.

⋆   ⋆   ⋆

The problem of Clara's performance at the 'Vangies had given Eleanor much troubled thought. The arrival of Miss Dene's letter concerning Martha seemed to present a possible solution.

Eleanor couched her request to Papa in general terms. 'Miss Dene is worried

about Martha. She needs encourage-
ment to work harder. I wondered if she
might take up singing, perhaps along
with Clara at the 'Vangies. They could
sing duets.'

Papa nodded approval, patting her
hand in a gesture that signified he
appreciated the interest she was taking
in her sisters.

It was arranged for the following
evening. Eleanor then asked permission
to visit Glasgow during the day to
purchase fabric for dresses for her
sisters. She did not mention she had
arranged to meet Lorne Fraser in the
city.

She completed her purchases in the
morning and caught a tram to the
Botanic Gardens. Waiting by the Kibble
Place greenhouses was Lorne.

'Come now and see my wonderful
new rooms,' he greeted her with a kiss
that sent her senses tingling.

Arm and arm they hurried along to a
terrace of biscuit-coloured stone houses
exquisitely elegant as suited Lorne. He

led her into a house in the middle of the terrace. 'My rooms are right at the top,' he whispered.

Lorne led her to a beautiful chaise lounge and then disappeared into an adjoining room which she assumed must be the bedroom. It was all very elegant and the furnishings were expensive. Dr Fraser must have spent quite a sum in providing this accommodation for his son.

When Lorne re-appeared he was carrying two glasses and a bottle of wine. 'My exams are over and I am as good as Dr Lorne Fraser at this moment,' he sat down beside her. 'Shall we drink a toast to that?'

The wine was deliciously cool and with a delightfully fruity taste. 'This is wonderful,' Eleanor was thrilled.

'Your first glass of wine?' Lorne looked amused.

She nodded. 'To you, Lorne,' she toasted him. 'For your success and future career with your father.'

He laughed. 'Forget that! I have no

intention of practising medicine in Kessog.' He pronounced the town's name as if it were the worst slum in all Scotland. 'I shall have a practice here with the best clientele in the West of Scotland.'

He re-filled her wine glass then held it to her lips. She sipped some, he tilted the glass and she continued to sip. Before she realised it the glass were empty again.

Lorne raised her to her feet and waltzed her round the room, causing her head to spin madly. Somehow they ended up in the other room. She was hazily aware of a large bed, covered in a patchwork quilt, although the room was dim and cool, the blinds having been drawn down.

'It is so cool and pleasant here,' she murmured as he gently sat her on the bed.

It was the sound of rhythmic banging which brought her senses surging back into control. It became louder and louder. Surely it couldn't be her head, fuzzy as it was, making all this noise? She tried to sit up and found she was swaying on the edge of the bed. How long had she been there? She looked round. She was alone in the room.

The noises were coming from the other room. The banging had ceased but now she heard loud voices.

'The exam results are posted!' someone shouted.

'Come at once, we want to read them together!' Another voice bellowed.

'Time to celebrate, Fraser!' A third voice joined in.

'Don't be stuffy. Of course you can come now. What's to keep you here?' The first voice demanded. 'Come on, man, I'll get your coat. Is it in the bedroom?'

Eleanor heard Lorne roar, 'No!' but by then the bedroom door had opened and a strange young man stood looking at Eleanor sitting on the bed. She saw a grin spread over the man's rosy face, then he bowed to her and closed the door with such exaggerated quietness that his voice was clearly carried back to her.

'Fraser! Another one! You naughty boy!

Having a reporter's mind could be something of a curse, Eleanor decided. It followed that she should be able to write down all that had happened that afternoon from the point of view of such a reporter's mind.

To begin, she would first detail the sequence. The meeting at Kibble Place, the happiness of two people being reunited after an absence, the whispered walk up the stairs to his new rooms. Stop! Her mind questioned the need for near silence. His fellow students hadn't bothered with that, shouting and banging all the way from the entrance. Of course! She was smuggled into his rooms. A concealment. A dark secret!

Followed by the endearments, the wine to toast success, the dance and then?

Now she understood exactly why

Doug Houston was so unreliable. How could someone report accurately on events if his, or her, mind was fuddled by wine or spirits? There had to be an omission in any such report. It would be an incomplete account of the event as the reporter could not be sure of all that had occurred.

As happened with me, she forced herself to admit. There was a sickness in the pit of her stomach that was nothing to do with wine.

She alighted from the tram which had taken her from the Botanic Gardens to the railway station. Lorne had wanted, begged, to accompany her to the station, to Kessog even. She had refused.

There was a long wait for the next train to Kessog but she sat on a bench oblivious to the hustle and bustle of the travellers. Thus she didn't notice Robina Insch, clutching a large bag and concealing herself behind a pillar so that Eleanor would not spot her. Robina wanted no questions concerning her unusual visit to Glasgow, or worse, the contents of the bag.

She arrived home to a raging row. 'What right have you to insist that Martha should sing with me tonight?' Clara blazed at her.

Eleanor gazed at her sister, knowing she had no fight left in her. Her plan had been conceived because she thought Clara was behaving in a cheap way. Now, who was she to judge? 'Martha needs to apply herself more. This seemed a good way to begin,' she said.

★ ★ ★

Since all his efforts to please Jeffrey had failed, Stephen decided that displeasing him might be more effective in imposing discipline. He announced he would accompany both Jeffrey and Amelia to the 'Vangies meeting.

Jeffrey's silent fury was palpable. Amelia, on the other hand, was delighted. 'I'm glad you're coming because Martha has to sing with Clara tonight. I shall be all alone.'

When they called at Gowanbank to collect the Paton girls, Stephen was delighted to find that Eleanor was going along too. He thought she looked tired and pale, but he had some news to counter that.

They walked together behind the youngsters. 'There has been a tremendous response to your report on Lily Ross,' he told her. 'Almost everyone supports your idea of a benefit fund to assist destitute widows.'

She replied quietly. 'Oh, I'm so pleased.'

It was such a lifeless response compared to her usual enthusiastic reactions that he cast around for a reason for her obvious despondency.

'Do you think we should allow Jeffrey and Clara to spend so much time together?' he asked. 'I'm not sure that Jeffrey is good enough for her.' He privately didn't think Clara was good enough for Jeffrey but he wanted to conceal his dislike of Eleanor's sister.

'I think the problem lies with our family,' she said, to his surprise. 'There's a lack of restraint, of judgement,' her voice trembled, then strengthened as if by tremendous effort. 'Of course, if we stop them meeting, we might have more trouble.'

'Yes, that had occurred to me,' Stephen conceded.

'I'd like to persuade Clara to take up a musical instrument, rather than concentrate on singing.'

Stephen hid a smile. Playing an instrument would lessen the opportunity for Clara to make an exhibition of herself. Clever Eleanor.

'Perhaps Jeffrey could be persuaded to join the Boys' Brigade,' she suggested. 'A company is about to be formed in Kessog. It is quite a disciplined organisation and concentrates on building the man through sport and other activities. That should appeal to him.'

'An inspired idea,' Stephen said, noticing at the same time that she was looking more cheerful.

The duet was a disaster. Martha stood like a frozen pillar beside the swaying and dipping figure of her sister. The congregation didn't know where to look.

Henry was waiting for their news when they returned to Gowanbank.

Stephen took his opportunity. 'Clara appears to have fine musical talent,' he said, noticing from the corner of his eye that the girl was preening herself at his remarks. 'It strikes me that she might play the flute, or some similar instrument. There is nothing so gracious or attractive as a fine young woman in command of such a refined instrument.' He despised his words and sycophancy, but, as he hoped, Clara's vanity rose to the occasion.

'Please, Papa, may I learn to play an instrument?'

Henry nodded and patted her golden curls.

'You won't have heard yet, Papa, but the Boys' Brigade company starting in Kessog is to have a band.' Eleanor said. 'The town will soon have many musicians.'

'You must join the Brigade, Jeffrey,' Clara cried. 'They drill and march and look so handsome in their uniforms. And we could make music together.'

Jeffrey, bemused, muttered some reply.

Stephen almost felt gratitude towards Clara. She had couched the Brigade's attractions in exactly the right terms to appeal to Jeffrey.

As they were saying goodnight at the front door, Stephen and Eleanor exchanged a triumphant conspiratorial look. 'It worked,' she said.

'Jeffrey will never suspect that I want him to join the Brigade,' Stephen said. 'I'll refuse to think about it for a day or so, and then give in. He will think he has outwitted me again.'

He was about to follow his brother and sister down the path when he turned back to Eleanor. 'Don't forget that this week's issue will have your report on the suffragettes. We're bound to receive many letters in response — good for circulation.'

Eleanor wasn't the only one looking forward to publication that week. That day Robina had been visiting a secret establishment in Glasgow in order to receive instructions on the properties and uses of inflammable substances. She had also purchased the relevant equipment.

She felt no remorse at betraying the specific wishes of her fellow members of the Sisters of Unity. Fine speeches and sincere intentions were all very well, but people who mattered, people with power to change things, paid no attention to those.

5

Euphemia Jamieson's spectacles were just level with the top of the net curtain which was tautly strung across the post office window. The curtain wouldn't have dared to sag. Its positioning allowed the post mistress to maintain constant observation of the square outside without having to move from her place behind the counter.

Euphemia probably knew more about the inner lives and secrets of Kessog than anyone else in town. However, her lips were sealed as securely as any love letter.

Love letters, at least two a day had arrived recently for Eleanor Paton and all post-marked Glasgow, all from Lorne Fraser, Euphemia guessed. It was well known in town that the pair were sweet on one another.

Euphemia hadn't noticed Eleanor

posting any letters in the box outside the office. A quarrel maybe? Time would tell.

Euphemia picked up the latest edition of the *Chronicle* and scanned the letters page. Often she was the first to see the latest edition, free to her, and could therefore anticipate if there would be an increase in postal business should any controversial subject be aired.

She raised her head as the door bell pinged and Robina Insch entered, although Euphemia had already spotted her crossing the square from the co-operative shop opposite.

'Have you seen the paper yet?' Robina asked with a friendly smile that was alien to her aloof personality.

'If it's printed, the newsboy will be selling it outside,' Euphemia knew the girl's ploy. She wanted to read the post office's copy without having to buy one of her own.

'You haven't read it then?' Robina

had noticed Euphemia slip her copy under the counter.

Euphemia noticed the intensity in Robina's light green eyes. The girl was excited about something. 'No,' she said.

'Do you close the post office when you have your dinner?' Robina leaned cosily against the counter.

Was the girl stupid? Everyone in Kessog knew that Euphemia lived in the back room of the post office and had never been known to turn away a customer whatever the hour. 'The hours of opening are engraved on the plate outside.' Euphemia smoothed her cuffs.

'I've noticed that there's always someone going in and out of the *Chronicle* office.' Robina sounded coy.

Euphemia thought there was only one way to interpret that. Robina was trying to get information about the newspaper men. It certainly wouldn't be Doug Houston, so she must have her eye on Stephen Walsh.

Well, she'd learn nothing from her.

Euphemia admired the new editor and didn't want him ensnared by the likes of Robina Insch.

'I have to get back to work now,' Robina said as if Euphemia had detained her. 'I hear Clara Paton is leading the singing at the 'Vangies.'

'At the moment, yes,' Euphemia was one of the members who wanted Clara silenced. Then it occurred to her that Robina must have heard that Stephen had been present at the last meeting.

She was still pondering Robina's schemes when she noticed that Eleanor had stopped the girl as she crossed the square. Euphemia was surprised that they knew each other beyond business in the shop, but their conversation appeared to be intense and serious. Surely to goodness Robina wasn't asking Eleanor about Stephen?

★ ★ ★

The first reaction to the newspaper item on the Sisters of Unity was not in fact a letter. Saturday was market day and Keir Square was usually crowded with stalls. That Saturday morning the stalls had crammed into High Street to avoid the *Chronicle* building.

The windows and front door were daubed and streaked. The walls were covered up to a depth of three feet and there was good ten inch pile fanning out across the square. The protest was obvious to any sensitive nose within a quarter of a mile.

'This is McAllister's work,' Stephen said to Doug as they stood in front of the pile of manure.

'Without a doubt,' Doug agreed, taking his pipe from his mouth. 'Mind you, the auld skinflint will regret the waste of money before the night's out.'

Stephen sighed. 'I'd better buy two shovels from the ironmonger.'

'Aye, and some stout bags,' Doug suggested. 'We can sell the stuff. It's market day and folk would be glad of some fertiliser. We can put the money to the Lily Ross fund and print that information next week.'

Stephen laughed and slapped Doug on the back. When the man was sober there was no-one to beat him for ingenuity and fast thinking.

From her vantage point behind the window of the co-operative shop, Robina smiled at the scene with anticipatory pleasure. The fight was on!

When he related the events to Eleanor and Henry later that day, Stephen was heartened to see the first smile from her in the last few days. 'We've sold every copy this week and it's only Saturday. Everyone wants to know what was so controversial,' Stephen told them.

Henry gave him a note requesting that he increase the print run for the next issue.

Stephen persuaded Eleanor to walk round the garden with him. 'I think it might be a good idea to respond to this hostile response with a follow up article detailing the funds the Sisters have collected for the poor.'

'Of course.' The idea seemed to cheer Eleanor. 'I will consult with Miss . . . ' she stopped.

'You can tell me her name,' he suggested. 'You can trust me.'

He was amazed by the look she gave him. Long and searching. 'I know I can trust you, Stephen,' her voice was low but sincere. 'But I did give a promise and someone trusts me to keep that.'

Eleanor broke some dead heads from flowers on the border. She was tempted to confide her suspicions about Robina Insch. None of the other Sisters thought she was a serious threat, but Robina's collaring of her in the square yesterday had unnerved her.

Why had Robina wanted to know details about the staff hours at the *Chronicle*? Stephen had cautioned her that someone might be using her. Was it Robina? But she could not fathom how.

Stephen watched the play of emotions over Eleanor's face. Something was troubling her. How he longed to take her hand, to make even the slightest physical contact. The only way he could show he cared, at the moment, was by helping her to develop as a writer. But that would hardly convey the tender love he felt for her.

'I plan to rent the house across the road, Fernlea, as our present home is too small for us. Would your father recommend me as a tenant?' he asked.

'Of course.' She smiled at him. 'He has a very high opinion of you.'

He longed for her to share that opinion, but he could only hope. He was still worried that the endearing spark was missing from her personality. He racked his brain trying to find out how he could help her. Maybe Clara was the problem.

'Are you going to the 'Vangies meeting this week?' he asked.

'I don't think so. Unless you think we should be there?'

He wanted to be with her, but not with another fifty people present. 'I don't think there's any need. The children are in safe hands.'

'I agree,' she said.

It was a decision they would both bitterly regret.

Eleanor's second article on the aims of the Sisters of Unity had more positive effects. 'Many letters contained money for the Sisters' work,' Stephen showed Henry his accounted statement.

Henry nodded and mimed shovelling.

Stephen laughed. 'McAllister is too mean to waste good manure twice. Any protest will all be on paper now.' But he was wrong.

On the following Saturday the market stalls were back in place. This time the protest didn't encroach on Keir Square. Instead it was emblazoned on the wall of the Chronicle's building in three-foot high white-washed letters which read:

SHRIEKING SISTERS

Robina Insch was possessed with cold fury when she saw the words, the common phrase which had been adopted by those against suffragism.

Now was the time to retaliate.

Mentally she ticked off the items of her plans. The physical means were hidden at home. Tuesday evening was the time she had chosen. The Post Office would be empty as Euphemia would be at the 'Vangies meeting.

To avoid being observed in the square she had decided to create a diversion. It was easy to persuade a local woman, for the price of a shilling, to barricade herself in the town's loom shop on that evening on the pretext of demanding equal wages with men.

She'd make enough noise to draw a crowd, and then of course Stephen Walsh would respond, hoping to cover a good story for the paper. That would get him out of the newspaper building. Doug Houston would already have left for the *Stag's Head*.

Robina counted the hours until Tuesday evening.

★ ★ ★

Eleanor had received another note from Miss Dene about Martha, and also stating she wished to discuss the Sisters' report in the paper. She stipulated Tuesday evening.

She had at last begun to shake off the despondency she'd felt since her visit to Lorne. His letters still came every day but she had not replied to any. She had nothing more to say to Lorne. While ashamed of her conduct, she realised that he did not care for her in the way she had hoped.

When the younger ones left for the 'Vangies, Eleanor decided to walk with them and then carry on to Miss Dene's cottage. She noticed that Jeffrey walked as close to Clara as possible while Martha said little or nothing in reply to Amelia's chatter.

Eleanor sighed. She couldn't police every place the children went and surely they would behave at the religious meeting house.

★   ★   ★

Robina had chosen Maggie Turner, a known troublemaker, to barricade herself into the loom shop and also paid her sister, Jean, to let the town know what was happening.

Jean began by telling everyone in the co-operative shop and then visiting all the establishments around the town.

From behind the shop window, Robina gloated as gradually all the townsfolk out at that time made their way to the loom shop. She saw Stephen leave the newspaper building.

Robina removed her apron. Seven o'clock. The shop was closing. Everything was falling into place. Two minutes later she was in her own house, unpacking hidden goods.

* * *

Doug was relieved that Stephen had gone to the loomshop. He was so tired. It had been a busy week with all the Sisters of Unity business and he needed to relax. He reached down from his chair and took a bottle from the waste paper bin where it was hidden. He'd just have a nip now and get along to the *Stag's Head* later. He jammed more tobacco in his pipe and lit up.

★ ★ ★

As soon as Eleanor left them outside the 'Vangies meeting hall, Clara announced, 'I'm not going in there. Carry on without me.' She walked off.

'I'm not going if you are not,' Jeffrey made to follow her.

'What about us?' Amelia wailed.

'Don't be a baby, you have Martha,' Jeffrey barely looked at them.

Amelia looked shocked and ready to cry.

'Wait until they are out of sight,' Martha whispered. 'We won't go either. Let's go back to your Aunt Ivy. She'll be furious that we've been abandoned and won't scold us.'

'Jeffrey will get into terrible trouble

for leaving me. Serves him right.'
Amelia followed Martha back along the lane.

★ ★ ★

'Go away, Jeffrey,' Clara drifted along the woodland path.

'That's the last thing either of us wants,' he tried to grab her hand. 'This was really clever of you, Clara, getting rid of the girls so that we could be alone.'

'Get your hands off me you impudent boy!' Clara twisted and flung away from him with a sudden and powerful movement.

Jeffrey staggered back, shocked and bewildered. 'But Clara, I thought you loved me,' he stammered.

'Love!' Clara spat out the word. 'If you dare to admire me, you will treat me with respect. I am special, not to be debased by a mere boy.'

Jeffrey was stunned. He was a 'mere boy' and she thought he would 'debase' her. All those months when he thought she cared. Every smile, every gesture from her had indicated that.

The force of her rejection stripped away all the pretence of enjoying her singing for the reward of a touch, a stolen kiss. She had looked silly with all her posing and aping of the music hall actress. At last he saw her for what she was, turned on his heel and left her in the woods.

The news telegraph came through just as Euphemia was locking the post office. She took it round to the newspaper office at once, but there was no response to her knocking.

Stephen always wanted telegraphs right away. She decided to take it to Meikle's Land. She would miss the 'Vangies meeting, but God would understand that duty came first.

Stephen was not at home but she left the telegraph and enjoyed a few minutes' chat with his Aunt Ivy. She was soon back in her premises, entering by the front door and locking the post office securely. She decided to leave the mail in the post box wire case until morning, her usual procedure.

Next door, Doug Houston twitched and mumbled in uneven sleep. He'd heard a noise earlier, but satisfied that it wasn't Stephen returning, he'd ignored it and taken another mouthful from the bottle and refilled his pipe.

Now his body slumped further down in the chair and his brain, fuzzy with a mixture of alcohol and exhaustion, failed to send messages to control the hands that held the bottle and the pipe. Doug's comforters slipped down, inch by inch, towards the full waste bin.

Outside, Robina re-entered the square and, passing the post office, casually dropped a bulky letter into the box.

Eleanor tried as tactfully as possible to alert Miss Dene to the possibility that Robina Insch could be a trouble-maker.

'She would never betray us,' Miss

Dene said with all her schoolmarm firmness.

'The *Chronicle* could not publish articles about the Cause if violence was involved,' Eleanor pointed out.

After a brief discussion over Martha's schoolwork, Eleanor left. She was somehow more than ever convinced that Robina presented some kind of threat. She decided to go and discuss it with Stephen in the office.

She set off down the lane. Waiting at the end was Lorne Fraser.

★   ★   ★

Duncan McAllister was repairing his barn. From his present position on the roof he had a clear view right over Kessog and it was a fine, clear evening.

His eyes narrowed. A wreath of smoke was curling lazily upwards, dirty grey against the clean washed blue of the sky. Given the direction it had to be from somewhere in the town square.

Maybe the post office or the newspaper building.

He thought of Euphemia Jamieson in the post office who'd put herself above the likes of a good, honest farmer when she'd refused to marry him twenty years ago.

Then there was that no-good Irish bog trotter with a thief for a brother probably in his office working on another piece about those suffragettes.

He had no call to help either of them. Let someone else call out the fire brigade. McAllister lifted up his hammer and resumed his work.

6

'Why don't you answer my letters, Eleanor?' Lorne's face showed none of its usual charm.

'Because I have nothing to say to you,' she continued walking.

'Stop, Eleanor. I have been waiting here for ages,' he sounded sulky.

'No time,' her voice, was coldly decisive. 'I have to go at once to the *Chronicle*.'

'At this time of night?' his anger glared. 'It's that Stephen Walsh you're off to see, isn't it? You didn't take long to replace me!'

'Don't be petty, Lorne. I have urgent editorial information to give him. My life is not all parties in the afternoon!' she flung at him.

'Eleanor, that afternoon . . . it wasn't what it seemed,' he tried to match her stride. 'Some friends held a party in my rooms one evening and . . . well, what was said to you was a joke. My friend was horrified afterwards at his coarse manners.'

Eleanor didn't bother to consider the lame explanation. 'Let me be, Lorne. I have no time for this.' She broke into a run.

Jeffrey returned home barely twenty minutes after Martha and Amelia. Aunt Ivy began to chastise him when Martha interrupted. 'Please don't be cross with him,' she said. 'We were the naughty ones, we didn't wait for him,' she gave Jeffrey a shy smile. 'I'm really sorry.'

She saw a flash of surprise cross his face.

'It was all Clara's fault, Jeffrey didn't know whether to follow her, or look after us. I must go home now,' she finished.

'Jeffrey will escort you this time,' Aunt Ivy pronounced.

Once outside, Jeffrey thanked Martha for her intervention, saying she had saved him from being chastised by both

Aunt Ivy and Stephen.

Martha made little of it, being thrilled just by being alone with him. He was so attractive, with his handsome face, tall figure, and the ever-present sense of tension, as if he was waiting for adventure.

'What's that smell?' he asked suddenly. 'It's smoke — look over there — belching into the sky.'

Martha looked where he was pointing. Dirty grey wreaths furled over the rooftops. 'Some old chimney,' she dismissed it. 'Now, tell me all about London. It must be so different to Kessog.'

Jeffrey's face lightened and he gave her a delightful smile. 'You are the first person who has ever thought I might be missing the old place,' he took a deep breath and began to tell her about his life there.

Stephen saw thick smoke rising above the rooftops as he hurried towards the centre of the town. Then he heard the clang of the fire bell and the clatter of the horses' hooves as the machine rumbled across the cobbles. Someone had called out the brigade.

He broke into a run and charged into Keir Square. His heart almost burst with fright when he saw smoke pouring from the first floor window of the *Chronicle* building. And then he remembered Doug was in the office when he left.

The firemen were breaking into the front door of the building and he was on the point of trying to follow them when he heard a scream. He saw Eleanor hurtling across the square towards him and he caught her in his arms.

'Is Doug inside?' her voice was hysterical.

'I don't know. I've been out . . . '

'Oh God, I'm too late,' she swayed in his arms and he held her close.

'Move back, move back!' The fire chief shouted at the onlookers who had suddenly crowded the square. Stephen noticed that the regulars who streamed out of the *Stag's Head* did not include Doug.

'Look at the post office!' someone in the crowd shouted.

Stephen saw what he'd thought was smoke swirling down from the newspaper building was actually coming from the post office. At that moment a fireman came out of the *Chronicle* building leading Doug, a smoke-begrimed, crumpled Doug, but alive.

Stephen and Eleanor pushed through the crowd to reach him. 'Thank goodness, you're all right,' Stephen said.

Above the din there came the clear sound of a window smashing. 'You didn't have to do that!' shouted Euphemia Jamieson to the fireman. 'I had it under control. It was only a little fire in the post box!' she gave them a glare and marched over to join Stephen and the others.

'Are you all right, Mr Houston?' she asked.

'Aye, aye,' Doug muttered.

'It was your smoke I smelt first,' Euphemia told him. 'Came out of my back door and looked up. I knew the amount of paper in your place so I went to the *Stag's Head* and got a boy to run for the brigade.'

'Are there two fires?' Stephen asked.

'There was one in my post box. Some bairns playing with matches, I don't doubt,' Euphemia said grimly.

By now the fires were completely extinguished. The stonework of both buildings was stained black.

The fire chief came over to talk to them. 'Small fires, both,' he said. 'But we probably just got here in time. No structural damage to either building.'

'Thank you for what you did,' Eleanor managed to say the appropriate words. 'We're very grateful.'

'Mr Houston here was the brave one,' the fire chief said. 'Had it not been for him, we might still be fighting your fire,' He patted Doug on the back and then called to his men to put the equipment back on the wagon.

'Come on, Doug, let's get you home,' Stephen said.

Eleanor was still gripping his arm with fierce intensity and he noticed how white she was. She appeared to summon a strength from somewhere as she said, 'I'm going to speak to Miss Jamieson.'

'I'll come back for you,' he promised. Something was seriously troubling her about the fire, although everyone was safe.

Half-an-hour later, he and Eleanor stood outside the *Chronicle* building. Stephen was full of apprehension. What would they find inside?

'Let's go in,' Eleanor was still tense.

An acrid smell hovered throughout the printing room but there was no visible damage to the machines and the wooden stairs to the offices were still intact.

The offices were in a dreadful state. The walls were blackened, as was the chimney breast. The desk in Doug's room was reduced to a charred wreck.

The metal waste paper bin lay twisted into a grotesque shape. A blackened whisky bottle lay among the ashes on the floor.

'Doug told me he must have fallen asleep with a bottle in one hand and his lit pipe in the other,' Stephen said crisply, kicking at the debris.

'You think Doug caused the fire?' Eleanor sounded surprised.

'What else?' Stephen was bitter. 'He was always careless with his pipe and now the drink finally got to his brain.'

'I thought it was arson,' she said.

'Arson?' he repeated with incredulity. 'Why would anyone commit that?'

'Then it was the post office that was the target,' she avoided his question.

'If you call boys playing with matches, arson, yes,' he felt a little irritated, then remembered her cry of, 'I'm too late.' What had she meant?

One look at her white, drawn face, made him decide to postpone asking her for an explanation.

'I'll clean up here as much as

possible. This week's edition must appear as usual,' he said.

'I expect it will take Doug a few days to recover,' she said.

'He can take months for all I care. I won't allow him to set foot in here, ever again.'

'You can't do that to him!' she cried out, colour returning to her face. 'The paper is all he has.'

'Then he shouldn't have thrown it away. The paper is all I have too, Eleanor,' he reminded her grimly. 'I don't drink when I'm here nor would I dream of smoking in a newspaper office.'

'We can all make mistakes,' she declared hotly. 'Doug's had a lot of troubles in his life.'

Stephen was astounded at her defence of Doug. 'You of all people, Eleanor, have seen the result of drink, especially on families. Think of the women you interviewed for your article on the temperance societies. You know perfectly well that drink ruins lives.'

'People do things under the influence of drink that they don't intend,' she murmured.

'I'm sure Doug did not want to reduce the *Chronicle* to ashes,' he tried to keep the sarcasm from his tone. 'But you can't pick and choose who to condemn and who to excuse.'

'It would be unfair to sack Doug. If the post office fire had taken hold he might have lost his life, and I bear some responsibility,' she said.

Stephen stared at her. What on earth was she talking about?

'I had a feeling that something dangerous was about to happen,' she shook her head wearily. 'I didn't know when or where. I was on my way back to the office to tell you when I saw the smoke.'

'What is this all about?' he asked softly. She was clearly distraught.

'One of the Sisters of Unity wanted to do something active to draw attention to the Cause,' she said.

He waited.

'I was wary of her, but I didn't mention it to you in case you wouldn't print my report,' she held her head up and met his eyes as she uttered her confession.

'The paper can not be seen to support militant action from anyone,' he said.

He gently sat her down in a smoke be-grimed chair and drew up another opposite her. She then went onto tell him about the anonymous girl's questions concerning the hours he and Doug worked at the office. And about her own call on the leader of the Sisters who refused to take her concerns seriously.

'If there was an arson attack, it certainly wasn't your fault,' Stephen said. 'If this woman was determined to do something, neither you nor I could have prevented it, so don't blame yourself. Actually, I would still have published the article because the Sisters believe in peaceful means,' he leant back in his chair and continued, 'Doug was responsible for our fire. If the fire at the post office was not due to small boys playing with matches, then it will have to be investigated.'

Stephen got up and did what he'd been longing to do for the last fifteen minutes. He lifted Eleanor to her feet and put his arms around her. Her head scarcely reached his shoulder and she buried her face in his rough jacket. There were no tears, only great racking sobs which seemed to echo in his own chest as she clung to him.

When she finally drew away she said, 'I seem to keep on doing irresponsible things, as if I've learned nothing.'

'Come on, Eleanor, you know that isn't true,' he strove to keep the tenderness from his tone. It was the wrong time to tell her how he felt. She was filled with guilt at the moment. 'Just remember that you can talk to me about anything at any time. I'm always here for you.' After a moment he suggested that they had to tell her father about the fire.

At Gowanbank, Henry was in his favourite armchair, Martha and Jeffrey sat in the window seat. Lorne Fraser was on sofa, a sulky look on his face.

Stephen quickly explained about the two fires. He assured Henry that the damage to their building was minimal. He also mentioned that Doug was responsible.

'Papa,' Eleanor went to her father. 'Doug made a mistake, but his first thought was to put out the fire, even before his own safety. The fire chief said he saved the building!'

Henry shook his head, his expression grim.

Stephen turned away but not before he saw Lorne Fraser rise hurriedly and cross to the fireplace, keeping his back to the room. But Eleanor was taking the defence of Doug too far. All this was because she still felt responsible.

'The paper is Doug's life,' she pleaded to her father. 'He's been loyal to you for years. Give him another chance.'

There was a long silence in the room, then Henry pointed at Stephen. This is unfair, he thought. Henry is avoiding making the decision.

'I know Doug as an excellent sub-editor,' he conceded eventually. 'If he stays I will have to accept it, but not the responsibility for his future actions.'

It sounded harsh and was meant to. But in truth Stephen had only given way on his real opinion in order to help Eleanor overcome her guilt.

Henry nodded his acceptance of Stephen's statement.

'I could help you clean up in your office tomorrow,' Jeffrey offered as he and Stephen walked home together. His brother volunteering to assist him? Although amazed, Stephen had the sense to accept without any questions. Any improvement in their relationship had to be a bonus.

'I'd rather not go to the 'Vangies again,' Jeffrey went on. 'Martha and I have a shared interest in foreign languages. I did think I would learn some if I joined the militia, but I know now that it is not the right thing for me. May I study French with Martha?'

Stephen, weary to the point of exhaustion, agreed. 'I hadn't realised that Martha is a charming, intelligent girl,' his brother said.

Stephen wondered what had happened with the pious Clara with whom Jeffrey had appeared so besotted. Oddly, Clara hadn't been present at Gowanbank. Lorne Fraser had and Stephen felt grim satisfaction as he recalled how the man had been ignored.

At that moment, Eleanor was trying to make Lorne quit the house. 'Come to Glasgow on Tuesday,' he injected a throb of passion into his voice.

Despite her weariness, Eleanor realised how shallow he was. The incident in his rooms would haunt her for a long time, but she also remembered his cruel and patronising view of the Kessog 'peasants' and how he would be too good a doctor for them.

Kessog was at the heart of her life and she cared deeply for all the people who lived there. Now she held open the front door for him to leave.

As she returned to the hall, Clara swept downstairs. 'I have no intention of returning to the 'Vangies,' she said. 'Jeffrey Walsh is an insolent pest. Kindly speak to Stephen about him.'

When they entered the parlour Martha was asking their father if she could study French. Papa looked relieved at her request, but frowned at Clara when she made a sound like a disdainful snort.

He caught Eleanor's eye and gave her a nod of approval. She guessed he was giving her credit, thinking it was her suggestion and thus being a good sister to Martha. She didn't deserve his good opinion. She was still deceiving him with her writing and had done little to guide Martha.

She felt a sense of despair, not only over her failure to prevent the fires, but in the double life she was leading, and how she had been deceived by Lorne.

Then, as she slid into bed she remembered that moment in the office when Stephen had held her. Once again, she had seen the caring, sensitive side of his character. Comforted, she fell asleep with the memory of his arms around her.

Next morning was devoted to cleaning up the newspaper offices. When Eleanor arrived she was surprised to find Stephen and Doug sitting in the editor's room evidently awaiting her arrival.

Doug immediately leapt to his feet. 'I'll not forget what you've done for me, Eleanor. Stephen told me that you insisted I kept my job.' His eyes were clear, although the effect of the previous night showed in his crumpled appearance and bearing. 'But I'll never let you down again.'

Eleanor saw the sincerity in his eyes and hoped it would be strong enough to overcome any temptations. He had learned, as she had, that not being in control was devastating. 'Come on, Doug,' she tried to sound off-hand. 'You know perfectly well I'd never have anything published if you didn't edit out my mistakes.'

Stephen entered the conversation briskly. 'I want someone to help clear up the mess here.'

'Lily Ross needs work,' Eleanor told him.

Eleanor slipped home again and asked Bethia to fetch Lily Ross. In fact, it would be a good idea if they had a regular office cleaner. Lily was the obvious choice although there was the problem of someone to look after her children.

Later in the day, she put the idea to Stephen and added, 'Since it is the school holidays, Martha and Amelia could look after Lily's children while she works.'

Stephen smiled at last. 'Good idea. Aunt Ivy will welcome some peace.'

'There's room for them all at Gowanbank, well away from Papa,' she said.

'I've secured the let of Fernlea and take entry this week,' he said. 'Perhaps the children could spend alternate days in each house.'

'And Jeffrey and Martha can work together. It seems they want to study French,' she said. 'It looks as if we've found a happy solution to some of our problems with the children, doesn't it?'

Stephen agreed. Neither knew that another devastating fuse had just been set.

Stephen's face became solemn again. 'While you were fetching Lily, we had a visit from the fire chief and the police sergeant,' he said.

Eleanor's stomach somersaulted and she waited with trepidation for his next words. 'Corrosive fluid was put into the post box last night, causing a small explosion, followed by fire,' Stephen maintained a neutral tone. 'Fortunately there were few letters in the box, although had the brigade not arrived when it did, it might have been very serious. There was nothing to identify who placed the device there, or why.'

'So it wasn't just boys playing with matches,' Eleanor's voice trembled.

'No, and the authorities want us to publish the information so that the culprit knows the crime has been discovered.'

Eleanor nodded. 'Will the guilty person be prosecuted?'

'Only if proof of identity can be found.'

'I gave a promise to the Sisters that their names would not be published,' she reminded him.

'Yes, but it is the responsibility of the Sisters to do something about the arsonist, if she is indeed one of them,' he paused. 'Perhaps you would also interview Miss Jamieson?'

She agreed, though the task was clouded with guilt and fear. As Eleanor expected, Euphemia was explosive in her reaction to the news.

'You mean someone planned to set fire to my post office?' she demanded.

'That appears to be the case,' Eleanor replied.

'I should have been at the 'Vangies last night,' Euphemia's eyes narrowed. 'If I hadn't taken that telegram to Mr Walsh's house the post office would have been empty at the time of the fire. So whoever put that device there knew my routine.'

'It would appear so,' Eleanor agreed tonelessly, thinking of the co-operative shop directly across the square with its clear view of the post office and the comings and goings of the post mistress.

Robina's questions to her regarding Stephen and Doug had been to ascertain if the newspaper office would also be empty. Clearly Robina had not intended to harm anyone, but that was no excuse.

Eleanor crossed the square and entered the co-operative shop. Robina was engaged in winding ribbons on to a bobbin. At first she pretended not to notice Eleanor, but raised her eyes when she heard her name. Eleanor at once noticed her defiant look.

'Did you hear about the two fires in the square last night?' Eleanor demanded.

Robina shrugged. 'Careless folk in this town keep the fire brigade busy all right,' she resumed her ribbon winding.

'Miss Jamieson is lucky to be alive,' Eleanor told her.

Robina's head jerked up. 'You mean she was in the post office at the time?' the girl's pale skin was robbed of every vestige of colour.

Eleanor nodded.

'But she always goes to the 'Vangies on a Tuesday,' Robina unwittingly gave herself away.

'Not last night,' Eleanor stared coldly at the older girl. 'She might have died if the fire had caught hold properly. And Doug was still in our office next door.'

Robina's hands twisted the ribbon and she refused to meet Eleanor's eyes. Eleanor left the shop, devastated that her suspicions had been correct. If only she had acted sooner and warned Stephen, but even then they might not have prevented it.

She went straight to see Miss Dene, told her of the fires and her confrontation with Robina.

'You did warn me, my child,' Miss Dene said with great sadness. 'And I dismissed your concerns. That was unforgivable. You are an intelligent girl and a credit to our cause.'

'No finger has been pointed at any organisation responsible for the fire,' Eleanor told her.

'Public opinion in Kessog will select us as the obvious target,' Miss Dene's face was white.

'We have no evidence, Miss Dene,' Eleanor reminded her. 'No-one saw who deposited the device in the post box.'

'No, she would be too clever to be spotted but I have no doubt that she is the culprit. I shall go directly now to the co-operative shop and tell her that by her actions she has jeopardised the Cause in Kessog.'

7

Eleanor passed her twentieth birthday without anyone noticing. The family had forgotten the date. It wasn't necessarily the date that was significant. She felt she had matured in many ways. Her earlier love for Lorne had withered to nothing and she accepted they would never have found happiness together. Their ideals were so different.

Her writing now took up so much of her life. The reports on the cause of the fire in the post office had resulted in some of the most vitriolic correspondence the *Chronicle* had ever received. The suffragettes were the target of most letters.

Stephen had been slightly withdrawn since the night of the fires. She longed to talk to him, not having forgotten that moment when he'd comforted her. The sense of security and warmth she'd experienced in his arms was an ever-present memory.

Then Lily Ross rushed into the office one morning. 'A tunnel has collapsed at the colliery. The women are gathering at the pit-head,' her face was creased with concern.

Stephen grabbed his jacket. 'Tell Doug where I've gone when he returns. I'll meet him there,' he said to Eleanor.

'He's gone to Newcrofts Hiring Fair and won't be back for hours,' she jumped up. 'I'll come with you.'

'No, it will be too distressing,' he barred her way.

'I know that,' she stared up at his long, lean face, trying to read his thoughts. 'I belong to this community. I want to help if I can.'

He looked at her for a long moment, then said: 'All right.'

The crowd had swelled to well over a hundred at the colliery entrance. There was a uniform sea of blackness, as it appeared to Eleanor. Women stood, huddled in shawls, some supporting babies, older children clutching at skirts.

A group of men crowded round the entrance, waiting for the cage to appear with colliers . . . news . . . whatever else there was to surface from the dark tunnels under the earth.

'Stand clear, the first cage is up!' a cry rang across the seething crowd.

Stephen looked in Eleanor's direction. 'Get back to the office,' he shouted, then immediately turned back to help with the stretchers.

Eleanor stayed where she was. She guessed he was trying to spare her from distress, but this was Kessog's disaster and she needed to witness what people were suffering.

As the injured were brought up and laid out on the stretchers she wondered if she would ever be able to forget those scenes. Would she ever find the right words to describe the suffering? She gave what comfort she could to the distraught families.

She waited until the last of the

miners had been taken away to hospital and then walked over to join Stephen. His clothes and face were smeared with coal dust and splashes of blood.

'You're still here,' he said wearily and then put his hands on her shoulders. 'I should have known you would stay to help. You are a brave girl.'

Despite her anguish at what she'd just witnessed, she felt a warm curl of pleasure at his praise of her.

As they left the colliery she noticed he was limping slightly. 'Lean on me. We haven't far to go,' she said.

It was late afternoon when they returned to the *Chronicle*. As Doug had not returned, Eleanor took over his desk, while Stephen sat in his own office, the door between the rooms being left open.

Her mind was still gripped with the horror of what she'd seen at the colliery. Powerless to help the victims there her only value lay in reporting the tragedy, and bringing the extent of the misery of the families to the attention of the townspeople in the hope that they would support them.

She and Stephen worked in tandem, as it were. While she wrote, Stephen was composing his editorial. Eleanor found she had some facts to contribute. 'The collier owner, Smeaton, is not known for spending money,' she told him.

'I can well believe that,' was his terse reply. 'The engine house equipment was outdated and some of the men told me that safety precautions were almost negligible.'

As ever, Henry was given the reports for his approval.

Grim faced, he read Stephen's editorial first and shook his head in anger at the relevant points which drew attention to Smeaton's heinous shortcomings as colliery owner. Then Stephen passed him Eleanor's reports, which carried no named by-line.

Again her father pointed at certain places, mainly the list of names of those injured.

'I was able to name those men I recognised when they were brought out . . . ' she began, then her voice trickled to silence when she noticed the massive frown appear on her father's face. She had given herself away by revealing her presence at the disaster and that she had written the report.

Henry pointed a long bony finger at the sheaf of reports, as if they were contaminated.

The time had come. 'Yes, those are my reports,' she confessed in a confident voice, contrary to her inner turmoil.

Papa didn't even look at her, but gave Stephen a stony glare, then pointed to the stack of *Chronicles* lying on a nearby table.

Stephen answered the implied question. 'Eleanor has contributed reports every week now for some time. You read and approved them.'

'I didn't set out to deceive you, Papa,' she stood firm, knowing she would lose everything if she showed weakness in front of him. 'I was the writer of the 'James Gillies' letters,' she saw his eyes flare with anger when he remembered how many he had printed. 'I wanted to prove to you that I could be a reporter.'

'The paper has benefited greatly from Eleanor's work,' Stephen sat down beside Henry. 'As have many good causes in the town which she has brought to the attention of our readers.'

Henry's hand released its grip on Eleanor's reports and they fluttered, page by page, to the floor. After a moment he gave Stephen a confirmatory nod, evidently exonerating him fully. He paid no attention to his daughter as she knelt to pick up the sheets of her work.

Disconsolate, she left the library and crossed to the dining room. Jeffrey and Martha, heads close together, were laughing over some translation.

Eleanor heard Stephen's footsteps in the hall and went to talk to him. 'Thank you for your support. I hope father hasn't blamed you, or worse, threatened dismissal.' She didn't want him to suffer on her account.

He smiled down at her, his dark, peat-coloured eyes warm with sympathy. 'No, nothing like that and,' he paused significantly. 'He hasn't told me to stop publishing your work, despite his being angry with you.'

A small victory. Life with Papa had never been easy for her, but now she could thole it better.

It was odd that when she had something too important to say the words flowed on paper, but now she was finding it difficult to express herself verbally. 'Thank you,' wasn't nearly enough to convey the warmth of her feeling for Stephen.

★   ★   ★

Eleanor's second visit to Colliers' Row was the most harrowing task she'd ever undertaken. She saw at first hand how even one week's loss of wages affected a whole family. Children were grizzling, hungry and scared, as they knew something was wrong. She gave each family some money from Lily Ross's original fund, which would surely run out shortly.

It was Bethia's day off and she decided to call in and see how her family were faring. Bethia's father lay in bed, wheezing, scarce of breath. Her mother, never strong in body or spirit, was sitting lifeless by the bed, crying. The young children were pale, blank-eyed, apathetic. Bethia was doing her best to keep the family together.

Eleanor drew the girl outside. 'Take some time off, you are needed here, far more than at Gowanbank,' she said. 'You won't lose any wages.'

Bethia bristled and said she'd come to the Paton house for a few hours each day. Eleanor knew better than to insist. Poor as they were, the Colliers' family hated the taint of what they saw as charity.

Eleanor moved into a downstairs room to be near Papa in case he needed assistance in the night and she did as much work as possible around the house to help Bethia.

Eleanor's time at the *Chronicle* was somewhat curtailed due to her extra duties, but one evening she stayed late to help Stephen with the enormous response to their articles on the colliery disaster. Money had poured in and they had to decide how to distribute it.

They walked home together in the cool of the September evening. They said goodnight as they reached the respective gates of Gowanbank and Fernlea. Indoors, Eleanor found Papa fretful and he wrote a note asking her to send Martha to him.

She walked slowly upstairs, aware the Clara was still practising with excruciating monotony. Martha's bedroom door was closed, not surprising in the noisy circumstances, and she had to knock loudly to be heard. Martha did not respond.

Sighing, Eleanor opened the door and went in. The room was in darkness and she thought at first that her sister was asleep. She lit the lamp and then stood stock-still.

Martha's room was empty, her bedcovers lay neatly unruffled. In fact, even the curtains were not drawn. Martha had not been in her room for hours, it seemed. So where was she?

Eleanor was now seriously concerned and her first instinct was to seek help from Stephen, although she knew Ivy had taken Amelia and Jeffrey to Glasgow.

As quietly as possible she slipped out to Fernlea. Stephen barely had time to register surprise when she blurted out: 'Martha is not at home. I can't find her.'

'She isn't here,' Stephen said. Eleanor was about to leave Fernlea when a gig drew up and Ivy and Amelia stepped out.

'What a day we've had!' Ivy greeted them. 'Glasgow is so busy but we had a wonderful time shopping. Just as well Jeffrey didn't come. He would have been bored.'

'Where is he then?' Stephen asked.

Ivy bustled into the house. 'Probably with Martha at your house, Eleanor.'

'They must have gone somewhere together,' Eleanor said as they left Fernlea. 'But where?'

'And why didn't they tell us?' Stephen's voice was full of anger.

Henry looked up in surprise as they entered the library. 'Martha appears to have gone out,' Eleanor tried to force a calm tone into her voice.

The thunderous cloud on Henry's face told them everything. He didn't like his daughters to defy him. He pointed to the ceiling.

But there was no need to call Clara. She sidled into the library. 'Did Martha tell you where she was going this evening,' Eleanor asked her sister.

Clara smirked. 'This evening? I don't think she mentioned this evening.'

Eleanor felt a chill of fear run right down her spine. Clara knew something! 'She went out earlier?' Eleanor asked.

Clara crossed to the window seat and draped herself on it. 'Quite some hours ago.'

Suddenly Henry rapped his table and pointed at Clara. Her head jerked up and she stared at her father. 'I overheard them. Planning,' she paused and then said with a triumphant little smile. 'They've run off to Gretna Green.'

'You wicked girl,' Eleanor shouted. 'You should have told us.'

Clara went to her father. It was only when she was by his side that she noticed he was purple with fury and he waved her away with an angry gesture. She ran from the room.

'I'll catch a train at once, then hire a gig for Gretna,' Stephen was already leaving the room.

Eleanor sat all night with Papa. His face had taken on a grey tinge and she was terrified he would suffer another seizure.

It was the longest night Eleanor had ever endured. When Bethia arrived in the morning, Eleanor explained.

'Oh mercy me, the poor children,' Bethia cried. Trust Bethia to take the compassionate view.

Eleanor took the opportunity of Bethia's presence to run into town and tell Doug that both she and Stephen would be delayed.

'Henry not so well?' he asked. 'Or problems with Jeffrey?'

'Yes, problems all round,' she said. It wouldn't do to broadcast the real facts as the reputations of both Martha and Jeffrey would suffer.

Stephen reached his destination on the last train going south and a hired gig took him to the village of Gretna. A small place, it didn't take him long to find out where Jeffrey and Martha had found lodgings.

'We were too late for a marriage today,' Jeffrey told him sullenly. 'It will have to be tomorrow.'

Martha sat in a chair, twisting a handkerchief in her hands.

'I think you know that this is wrong,'

Stephen strove to keep calm.

'We love each other,' Jeffrey burst out.

'Yes, I can understand that,' his brother replied. 'I'm not condemning you for that, but if you were to marry here, you would be outcasts in Kessog society. It is not the accepted way of starting a life together. It would be altogether more difficult for you.'

Jeffrey stared at his brother in surprise. Stephen knew he had expected anger and condemnation, not understanding.

'I suggest it would be better if you both returned with me and explained how much you care for one another and that you would like to marry — sometime in the future, with the blessing of your families,' he concluded.

Jeffrey took Martha's hand and gazed into her eyes. Then they both nodded. Stephen concealed his enormous relief.

They caught the first train back to Glasgow the following morning but even then it was mid-afternoon before they arrived back at Gowanbank.

A white-faced, exhausted Eleanor met them at the door. She immediately took Martha in her arms. Stephen's heart lifted at her instinctive gesture. She was of the same mind as himself. The youngsters were not old enough to realise what distress they had caused.

They all went into Henry's library. 'They are not married,' Stephen said immediately.

Henry's head was sunk on his chest and for a moment Stephen thought he'd taken ill again, but then he realised the older man couldn't bear to look at them.

'Papa . . . ' Martha began in a wavering voice.

Henry raised an arm and pointed to the door.

'I want to apologise, sir . . . ' Jeffrey began.

The arm jerked up again.

'Go back to Fernlea, Jeffrey.' Stephen said and the young pair left the room.

'Jeffrey's only concern is Martha,'

Stephen said to Henry. 'He knows it was wrong to run away but they do love each other and would like to marry in the future.'

Henry Paton raised his head. A look of outrage on his face. He reached out for his pad and pencil.

'No, Papa!' she cried. 'You can't do this to Stephen. He is not to blame!'

But Henry held out the slip of paper and motioned to Stephen to take it. It said, *You are dismissed from your post.*

Stephen knew it was useless to protest. Henry was reacting with anger and retribution with some justification. After all Stephen was responsible for Jeffrey. He caught Eleanor's eye and shook his head slightly to indicate that he would do nothing at the moment.

8

Within days, Henry's brother-in-law, Charles Cleland, had found a new editor for the *Chronicle*, although he thought Henry had made an error of judgement in dismissing Stephen Walsh. The young Irishman had set a new seal of professionalism on the paper, better even than when Henry was editor, and it was petty to make him suffer for his brother's waywardness.

Morris Barnton had been suggested to Charles by a fellow banker. Charles didn't take to Barnton, evidently recently resigned from editing a weekly newspaper in the North East. He found him arrogant and opinionated, but since the situation was urgent he had no choice but to appoint him.

Barnton swept into the *Chronicle* office. He was overtly polite to Eleanor, only because she was the owner's daughter she guessed, but he treated Doug with near contempt.

He at once began rejecting some of Eleanor's reports, claiming lack of space in editions. She guessed that he would gradually edge her out. Surprisingly, she realised she didn't care too much, although she hoped Doug wouldn't suffer the same fate.

Not an hour passed, but she thought of Stephen. Thought how she had taken him for granted all those months when he'd supported her, gently guiding her to seek truth and balance in her writing. How could she have undervalued him so?

She thought of his gentle face, hair that was often untidy because he never spent time attending to himself. Of his hands, forever ink-stained, but so tender holding hers. How could she have been so blind to the goodness and strength of the man and wasted her time and love on the worthless Lorne Fraser?

Uncle Charles had found Stephen's

family a tenement flat not far from his own in the west end of Glasgow. 'Your father should let Jeffrey visit Martha. It's cruel to keep them parted like this,' Aunt Flora had said on a recent visit to Gowanbank.

It was true that Martha seemed to have lost all her spirit and energy. She was lost without Jeffrey. *Just as much as I am,* she admitted to herself, *without Stephen.*

Stephen picked up the *Chronicle* and read it again. He could find nothing written by Eleanor. Here and there he spotted Doug's reporting style but the rest appeared to be the new editor's work. And it was appalling.

Stephen was grateful to Charles Cleland for finding him a post with a Glasgow daily newspaper. It kept him busy. But not enough to stop him thinking constantly of Eleanor.

How he longed to see her again. It was some comfort that Eleanor's Aunt Flora had struck up a friendship with Aunt Ivy. He clung to the hope that one day Eleanor might be permitted to visit her Aunt in Glasgow, although he had heard that Henry had forbidden his daughters to leave Kessog.

The opportunity to call on Charles Cleland came sooner than expected. Some of his new colleagues on the Glasgow paper had told him that Barnton was considered to be something of a charlatan.

It appeared that he changed jobs about every six months and after he left each newspaper, which was then on the point of failing, it was bought over by another company. Charles should know of this. He would visit him on Wednesday evening.

★ ★ ★

Although Henry had not suffered another seizure as a result of Martha's escapade, he slowly began to lose interest in many things. When Eleanor rather timidly suggested that she take Martha to visit her Aunt Flora, he agreed without demur.

Eleanor hoped the trip would restore some colour to Martha's cheeks and took her shopping. In the afternoon they had tea with Aunt Flora who was distressed at Martha's appearance.

'The child needs a change of air. I shall ask Henry if I may take her to our summer residence at Cove for a few weeks,' she said.

Eleanor thought it a good idea and they kissed their aunt goodbye.

'Will you come to Cove too, Eleanor?' Martha asked as they made their way to the tramway halt.

'I can't leave the paper at the moment,' she said.

'Don't leave me with Papa and Clara,' Martha pleaded.

'Martha, you must learn to stand up for yourself. You are a clever girl and you are important to me, and to Jeffrey. Remember you are an individual, your own person, never forget that.' It sounded preachy and harsh and Eleanor decided to reveal a secret

166

whispered to her by her aunt. 'You must tell no-one at home, but Aunt Flora intends to invite Mrs Dunkers, Amelia and Jeffrey to Cove,' she told her.

At that moment Stephen alighted from the tram and began to make his way to Charles Cleland's house. Within minutes he met the two girls walking towards him. His heart almost stopped. Eleanor and Martha.

'Hello, Stephen.' There was a breathless quality to her voice and he saw a light come into those lovely green eyes and watched a slow blush colour her cheeks. They stared at each other for a moment until a rustle broke the silence.

'And Martha,' he went on lamely. 'How are you both?'

Eleanor never knew what she replied. All she was conscious of was wanting to reach out and touch him — his shoulder, his hair, hold his hand, and be enfolded in his arms.

All the longing of the past few weeks crystallised into aching desire. Her limbs seemed lifeless while at the same time every nerve in her body was tingling. And she knew she'd lost her heart to Stephen.

The bell of the tram clanged at the stop and they had to climb aboard. There was no time for more words, but Eleanor held out her hand. Stephen caught it with his and he knew he hadn't lost her after all.

★   ★   ★

Papa listened to Eleanor's request that Martha be allowed to stay with Aunt Flora at Cove. 'I have also secured Clara a position as pupil teacher with Miss Dene,' she said.

He hid his true reaction from his eldest daughter and indicated his agreement to both proposals. It wouldn't do to reveal the relief he held that the younger girls would be out of sight for a while. Guilty relief, albeit. He had promised his late wife to take care of the girls and had failed dismally. Clara was nothing more than a hypocritical vain girl, Martha weak and empty-headed.

Eleanor was the only one who had matured into an admirable person. She could write, although he'd never tell her so. He still wasn't happy that his daughter was working for a wage on a newspaper.

He was almost certain too, that he was going to lose the *Chronicle*. The Barnton man was turning it into a rag. Dismissing Stephen Walsh had been a catastrophic mistake.

He summoned his strength and gave Eleanor a note for Barnton, demanding that he visited Gowanbank. When she handed it over later, Barnton pursed his lips. 'Sometime next week.'

'Today, if you will,' Eleanor said in the tone of a proprietor's daughter.

'Well done.' Doug laughed quietly after Barnton had stormed out of the office. Barnton had scarcely crossed the square when two gentlemen presented themselves in the office. They introduced themselves as Calcutt and Davidson, business associates of Morris Barnton.

'He is unavailable at the moment,' Eleanor said, immediately wary of the pair. 'But since I am the proprietor's daughter, you can discuss any business with me.'

The men exchanged what only could be described as furtive looks and announced they would return later.

'Do you think they were applying for positions here?' Eleanor asked Doug after they had gone.

'Dressed like that? No inky fingers for a start and too well fed looking for journalists,' Doug said. 'By the way, I went up to Glasgow yesterday to see Stephen in his new position.'

Eleanor's heart raced, but she guessed Doug's visit had nothing to do with her.

'He's having a word with your uncle about Barnton. Seems there's been some odd rumours about him. Stephen wants me to let him have a copy of the accounts. Is that all right with you?'

'Of course, Doug. Let's get them out now while Barnton's away.'

They took the accounts file from the safe and Doug tied it in a parcel. 'If Barnton notices they're missing, I'll say my father wanted to look after them,' she said.

'Good idea,' Doug said, then patted his jacket pocket. 'I almost forgot, Stephen gave me a letter for you, probably explaining all this.'

Trying to disguise the tremble in her hands, Eleanor took the letter, then opened it as Doug was clearly expecting her to do. The words danced before her eyes. She slipped the letter into her skirt pocket, but each word was imprinted on her senses.

The letter read, *I have so much I want to say to you that it cannot wait. I love you with all my heart. Can we meet in Glasgow on Saturday?*

November fog was shrouding the West of Scotland on Saturday morning. Stephen was relieved that he'd sent a message via Doug that Eleanor should remain in Kessog. They'd meet there as he was going to Gowanbank. He now had enough information to convince Henry that Barnton was not to be trusted.

He caught the first train from Glasgow. It drew warily into Kessog station. Stephen knew that fog was only part of the problem. Doug had told him that the Irish gangers laying the new line between Kessog and Newcrofts were demanding their due money now. The contractor wanted the whole line to be completed by Christmas and then wages would be paid. The gangers' families could not wait that long.

Stephen jumped out as soon as the train stopped and started off for Gowanbank, unaware that Eleanor was in the station waiting room, ready to catch the train back to Glasgow. Doug had forgotten to pass on Stephen's message.

Bethia gave Stephen a warm smile when he arrived at Gowanbank. 'Oh, it's right good to see you again, Mr Walsh, but everyone is out except Mr Paton,' she said.

Stephen felt assured that Eleanor must have gone to the *Chronicle* office. He'd catch up with her there.

Henry stared at him, unsmiling, when Stephen entered the library. 'I have some disturbing information about Morris Barnton,' Stephen said without preamble.

An alert look immediately came into Henry's eyes.

Firstly, Stephen presented the accounts which Doug had brought him.

Stephen himself had been shocked to see that Barnton had laid off two of the best printers, citing lack of work. Only three months before, Stephen had taken on extra printing, outwith the newspaper's requirements, in order to boost income. It appeared that Barnton had cancelled those contracts.

Henry immediately realised, as Stephen had done, that the newspaper business was losing money. Stephen then went on to relate the information he'd been given over Barnton's previous appointments. How each one had ended after only a period of six months, after which the newspapers involved, due to lack of circulation and finance, had been forced to sell out to a larger conglomerate.

Henry was now frowning. He took out his pad and wrote on it. *He's reduced the Chronicle to a rag, but pays no attention to my instructions.*

'That's how he appears to have destroyed other newspapers,' Stephen commented.

He has a three-month contract. What's to be done? Was Henry's next note.

Stephen's first reaction was that Henry was putting trust in him. It gave him a sense of quiet elation. No matter what had happened over Jeffrey and Martha, Henry still recognised him as a good newspaperman.

'I have details of his past employment which he naturally did not make available to Mr Cleland when he was appointed. Nothing can be proved, of course, but our knowledge might just be enough to frighten him off. Shall I fetch him from the office?'

Henry nodded vigorously.

When he reached the *Chronicle* office, Stephen was dismayed to find that Eleanor was not there. Instead, two men were in close discussion with Barnton.

Barnton glared at Stephen's entrance and did not deign to introduce the men. 'Mr Henry Paton, the proprietor, wishes to see Mr Barnton at his home now on urgent business.' Stephen bowed to the men.

As he expected, the two men hurriedly left the office.

'What's all this about? Paton can't discuss anything,' Barnton snapped at Stephen.

'Business,' was his reply. 'And I will speak for him.'

Barnton made a great show of pompous bravado, but Stephen ignored it.

Back at Gowanbank, Stephen presented all his evidence to Barnton. The man blustered then denied everything, then told Henry that his paper was worth nothing.

'And that's why Calcutt and Davidson were in the office — to buy it up?' Stephen said.

Barnton's face seemed to shrivel as it dawned on him that Stephen had indeed made a thorough investigation of his past practices and knew of his involvement with the two men who acted for the conglomerate.

'Either we take this to our legal representative or it is mutually agreed that your contract is terminated as of now.' Stephen gave him no chance to recover.

Barnton threw out a few blustering epithets but he realised the game was up and he abruptly left the house.

Henry rose to his feet and held out his hand to Stephen. They shook hands and then Henry pointed to the pile of *Chronicles* on the side table. He looked at Stephen enquiringly.

He was offering him the editorship.

'I'd be honoured to return,' Stephen told him.

Henry smiled, possibly for the first time in a long while.

'Is Eleanor about?' Stephen then asked.

Henry resorted to his notepad again. *Gone to Glasgow.*

Stephen hid his acute disappointment — and worry. This was no day to be travelling when the fog was so bad. He glanced at his fob watch. By now she would have discovered he was not at home and would probably be on the way back to Kessog.

'I'll meet her off the train,' he told Henry and left the house.

Eleanor called at Stephen's house in the West End, but there was no reply to her knock. She was unaware that her Aunt Flora had invited Ivy, Amelia and Jeffrey to Cove for the weekend.

She was sensible enough to realise that something important must have delayed Stephen or that they had unknowingly passed each other in the fog. She then went to his newspaper office where one of his colleagues told her that he'd gone to Kessog to follow up some dispute there.

At once, she realised he must have some information about Barnton and she hurried back to the station.

It was a slow, tedious journey as the fog was even thicker than earlier. Eleanor was in the grip of impatience. How desperately she wanted to see Stephen.

The railway engine glided through the fog into Kessog station with its tender and two carriages. The driver peered through the gloom trying to judge how far the train was from the buffers. Nobody had remembered to tell him that the engineers had instructed the gangers to remove the buffers earlier in order that the last remaining lines of track could be laid to connect Kessog with Newcrofts.

The lines of track had not been laid.

And wouldn't be until the gangers had been paid.

Stephen moved to the very edge of the platform to scan each carriage window for a glimpse of Eleanor.

The engine brakes screeched but the train did not stop. With horror, Stephen realised that the driver had not been told about the missing buffers.

Suddenly he saw Eleanor peering through a carriage window. He grasped the handle of the compartment door, yelling, 'Get out! Everyone get out!'

He tried to turn the handle but at that point the train ran off the rails and slowly, inexorably, began to tilt towards him and he lost his balance.

Eleanor was almost thrown off her feet but she had managed to grasp the inside handle and now flung herself against the door. When she got out she saw Stephen lying where the track should have been. The carriage teetered again. She screamed for help and a score of gangers appeared alongside the carriage, supporting it from collapsing on Stephen.

Eleanor crawled down beside him, together with two men and they tried to ease Stephen up from the track.

Stephen could feel nothing below his right elbow. He was unaware that he was drifting in and out of consciousness. He tried to speak, but all he could hear was Eleanor's voice.

'Yes, my dearest. I know you do and I love you too. I'm not leaving here without you. Nobody will part us again.'

★ ★ ★

'You're a lucky man, Walsh.' Dr Fraser sat on a chair by Stephen's hospital bed next day. 'I thought your right hand was done for, but your two broken fingers will mend. You'll live to write many an editorial yet.

'That carriage could have fallen on you. You wouldn't be here today if that had happened. I reckon your rescue party saved the day.' Dr Fraser paused.

'And here she comes now.'

Stephen turned toward the ward entrance. Eleanor was approaching. He remembered every touch and word of hers from the previous night. All the energy and passion that so characterised her, was now for him alone.

They only had to look into each other's eyes to see all the love and devotion and promise for the future and then to hold each other with a longing and intensity long denied.

THE END

We do hope that you have enjoyed reading this large print book.

Did you know that all of our titles are available for purchase?

We publish a wide range of high quality large print books including:
Romances, Mysteries, Classics
General Fiction
Non Fiction and Westerns

Special interest titles available in large print are:
The Little Oxford Dictionary
Music Book, Song Book
Hymn Book, Service Book

Also available from us courtesy of Oxford University Press:
Young Readers' Dictionary
(large print edition)
Young Readers' Thesaurus
(large print edition)

For further information or a free brochure, please contact us at:
Ulverscroft Large Print Books Ltd.,
The Green, Bradgate Road, Anstey,
Leicester, LE7 7FU, England.
Tel: (00 44) **0116 236 4325**
Fax: (00 44) **0116 234 0205**

Other titles in the
Linford Romance Library:

TO CAPTURE A HEART

Karen Abbott

When Gill Madison visited the
beautiful Malaysian island, Langkawi,
at the end of a backpacking holiday,
she knew she would love to spend
more time there. Being on the spot
for an offer of a 'Girl Friday' job on
board a pleasure boat seems to good
an offer to turn down, especially
when the skipper is as handsome as
Bart Lawson. However, Gill soon
discovers that it isn't all to be plain
sailing.

FATEFUL DECEPTION

Kate Allan

When Captain Robert Monceaux, of the Fifteenth Light Dragoons, rescues Miss Lucinda Handscombe from a highway robbery, she piques his interest. Robert cannot stay away from her, and Lucinda becomes attracted to him. When her guardian demands that she accompanies him to Madeira against her will, Robert offers to save her. But, after a misunderstanding, Lucinda runs away. And when Robert eventually finds her, they realise they must learn to trust each other for their future happiness together.

GROWING DREAMS

Chrissie Loveday

After the death of her long-absent ex-husband, Samantha Rayner and her young daughter Allie move to Pengelly in Cornwall to start afresh. When they stumble across the overgrown grounds of Pengelly Hall, Sam starts dreaming of restoring them to their former glory. Jackson Clark, the business-minded owner of Pengelly Hall, agrees to fund the project, but could Sam have taken on more than she bargained for . . . And what secrets does head gardener Will Heston hold in his past?

MAIL ORDER BRIDE

Catriona McCuaig

Lydia McFarlane has been used to a life of wealth and privilege, but when her father remarries, her new stepmother starts a systematic campaign to remove Lydia from the family home in Ontario, plotting to marry her off to a man who doesn't love her. Lydia decides to take matters into her own hands, and runs away to the prairie town of Alberta to become a mail order bride — but life in the Golden West is not as idyllic as Lydia has imagined . . .